DREAMS THAT WON'T LET GO

Books by Stacy Hawkins Adams

Speak to My Heart

Nothing but the Right Thing

Watercolored Pearls

Jubilant Soul

The Someday List

Worth a Thousand Words

Dreams That Won't Let Go

JUBILANT SOUL
BOOK THREE

DREAMS THAT WON'T LET GO

A Novel

Stacy Hawkins Adams

a division of Baker Publishing Group
Grand Rapids, Michigan

Published by Revell
a division of Baker Publishing Group
P.O. Box 6287, Grand Rapids, MI 49516-6287
www.revellbooks.com

Printed in the United States of America

Library of Congress Cataloging-in-Publication Data
Adams, Stacy Hawkins, 1971–
Dreams that won't let go : a novel / Stacy Hawkins Adams.
p. cm. — (Jubilant soul ; 3)
ISBN 978-0-8007-3268-4 (pbk.)
1. African Americans—Fiction. 2. Families—Fiction. 3. Conduct of life—Fiction. 4. Texas—Fiction. I. Title.
PS3601.D396D74 2010
813′.6—dc22 2009042836

Published in association with the literary agency of The Steve Laube Agency, 5025 N. Central Ave. #635, Phoenix, AZ 85012-1502.

10 11 12 13 14 15 16 7 6 5 4 3 2 1

To Sharon Shahid, Muriel Miller Branch, and Carol Jackson
for your ever-present encouragement, friendship, and love

There is no fear in love. But perfect love drives out fear, because fear has to do with punishment. The one who fears is not made perfect in love.

1 John 4:18

1

Indigo Burns loved her brother—just not today.

Today, she wished Reuben would go home to Seattle. Today, she couldn't deal with his upstaging her. She needed just two hours of Mama's time, to treat Mama to lunch and ask her advice.

Never mind that she was a self-sufficient adult with a job, her own place, and two degrees; she still trusted Mama's wisdom—craved it—when she needed to make decisions this big.

But instead of enjoying the atmosphere in Jubilant's new casual chic dining spot with Indigo, Mama was calling her from home, sounding like a breathless schoolgirl.

"Looks like I'm going to be late, baby," Mama said. "Reuben left to run an errand this morning, and he's on his way back to the house. He called and asked me to stay until he gets here. He has something to tell me. You don't mind, do you?"

Indigo clamped her lips together. She couldn't tell Mama that she did mind, or that she didn't understand why Reuben's wishes always trumped everyone else's.

Mama kept chattering, as if she didn't expect a response. "I don't know what that boy is up to, but I told him to hurry. Can you give me fifteen minutes? Go ahead and order my iced tea."

"Alright, Mama," Indigo said after a long pause. "See you when you get here."

She clicked off the cell phone and took a deep breath so the tears she felt forming would dissipate. Being a crybaby wouldn't help. Why was she so emotional anyway? It was just lunch, and Mama hadn't canceled.

As much as she wanted to dismiss the resentment, though, it persisted. That "boy" wasn't a boy. He was a man. A husband. A father. And every time he came to visit, the world didn't have to stop.

But it always did.

Indigo's stomach rumbled. Hunger and frustration were not a great combination. The menu images and descriptions of supersized salads, sandwiches, pasta, and gourmet burgers, coupled with the aromas wafting from the plates of nearby diners, didn't help.

Her phone rang and she was thankful for the distraction. She picked up on the second ring when Shelby's number and smiling cocoa brown face flashed across the screen.

"What's up, Mrs. Pappas?"

"That's Lieutenant Pappas to you, girlfriend. How many times do I have to tell you that?"

"You can fly naval helicopters all you want, but when you come home every night, you're still Hunt Pappas's wife, Ms. Thang," Indigo said.

"And glad about it." Shelby laughed. "Where are you? What's that noise I hear in the background?"

Indigo sighed and glanced at the door, where a hostess was greeting new diners. "Sitting here at The Bend, waiting on Mama, and hating on Reuben."

"Indie—"

"He flew into town last weekend for Daddy's birthday and decided to stay for the week, since his bosses at Amazon.com allow him to telecommute. Wonder how Peyton and his little man feel about being stuck in Seattle while he's here, hanging out with his parents."

"What happened this time?"

"Mama is supposed to be joining me for lunch. I have some exciting news that I need to get some feedback on—that's why I left you a message too. But apparently Reuben left the house this morning for a while, and the minute he called and said he needed to talk to her, Mama dropped her keys and purse and set up a vigil near the front door."

Shelby laughed. "You think she found a spot on the floor and sat Indian style?"

Instead of joining in, Indigo tightened her grip on the phone and clenched her teeth.

"Come on, Indie," Shelby said into the silence. "Lighten up. You helped Reuben reconnect with the family four years ago. Now you get upset every time he comes home to spend time with your parents and the rest of the family, and you treat him like an ex-con. Why are you so resentful . . . so jealous?"

Only Shelby could find the courage to ask her a question like that. Indigo handled it her usual way, by asking one of her own.

"Are you going *Dr. Phil* on me? Has that talk show guru been on the Corpus Christi naval base or something?"

"Good comeback, Indie, but stop dodging the question."

Indigo perched an elbow on the table and rested her chin in her palm. She gazed out of the draperied windows at the restaurant's landscaped lawn and expansive parking lot. Shelby was right:

she was swimming in envy and anger, and the two bedfellows didn't suit her.

Indigo was thankful Reuben had stopped distancing himself from the family and that he now visited Jubilant several times a year. But she hated how whenever he came to town, Mama and Daddy decided everything and everyone else could wait.

The fact that both her best friend and her fiancé kept giving her the same lecture rattled her. Max continuously urged Indigo to deal with how she felt about Reuben's return, and to understand that Mama had enough love for her, Reuben, and their sister, Yasmin, even when Mama got caught up in "Reubenmania."

Max and Shelby might be right; but she was human. It hurt.

Indigo scanned the café, noting the smiling couples and small groups of diners, some dressed casually with others suited up for business, and decided she wasn't going to feel self-conscious if she wound up eating alone. She was hungry, and in all of the excitement over Reuben, Mama might not show.

"You're right, Shel." She sat upright and tucked a strand of loosely curled, shoulder-length hair behind an ear. "I need to pray about how I've been feeling—"

"And acting."

"Maybe I'm being immature, but when the truth is right in front of you, and it makes you feel like an outsider in your own family, it's hard." Indigo sat back in the chair and sighed. "Let me go so I can stop whining, okay? I'll call you later to share my news. I've got to order something to eat so I can get out of this restaurant."

"Alright, Indie. Love ya."

Indigo laid the cell on the table and motioned for her waitress. She was about to request the chicken club pita with cucumber yogurt sauce when she looked up, out of the window, and saw Mama's blue Toyota Avalon pull into a parking space right in front.

“Here’s my mom, now,” she told the waitress. “Give us five minutes?”

Indigo pushed her chair back and stood to greet Mama. Her face fell when she saw that Mama wasn’t alone. Reuben held open the door and followed her inside.

Mama greeted her with a hug.“I made it! Reuben hadn’t eaten either, so I insisted that he join us.”

Reuben draped his arm around Mama’s shoulders and smiled. “Can we fit another chair at the table, sis?”

Before she could respond, the waitress materialized and pulled one over.

“Here you go, sir. What would you like to drink?”

“Thanks,” Reuben said. “I’ll have a Dr Pepper.”

He waited until Mama and Indigo were seated before sliding into a chair himself.

Mama sipped her now iceless tea, then reached over to pat Indigo’s hand. “You look pretty, today. I love that purple top.”

Indigo smiled and squeezed Mama’s hand.

“Thanks, Mama. You’re looking nice too.”

She had been itching to tell Mama what was on her mind, but now that Mama was here, Indigo wasn’t sure she wanted to, with Reuben joining them.

“Want to order?” Indigo asked when she noticed the waitress hovering nearby. “Mama, are you getting your usual—a Cobb salad and a bowl of clam chowder soup?”

Mama laughed. “Why not? At my age, it’s about enjoying what you love.”

Indigo shook her head. Mama was always calling herself old, but had no problem catching the eye of men her age and younger. Her cinnamon skin was smooth, her figure was slim, and she lit up a room with her energy, her lively eyes, and her warm smile.

"I keep telling you, seventy-something is the new sixty-something."

Before Indigo could wave over their waitress, Mama continued. "Well, today I'm going to surprise you and order something different. I'm feeling adventurous. Reuben just made me the happiest mother and grandmother in the world." Mama beamed at him. "Do you want to tell her, or can I?"

Reuben chuckled and shrugged. "Go for it."

Mama's eyes danced. "Reuben's been offered a job here in Jubilant. He, Peyton, and Charles David are moving home!"

Indigo's breath got caught in her throat. Tears erupted before she could stop them, but Mama misunderstood her weeping. She grinned and grabbed one of Indigo's hands.

"I know, sweetie! I was so happy, I cried too."

Indigo swiped her wet cheeks with a thumb and glanced at her brother. The tears had blurred her vision, but she could see past them enough to recognize the emotion swimming in Reuben's eyes. She was startled. Instead of the pride or joy she had expected, she saw fear. This was a defining moment for the ever-perfect Reuben. Why on earth was he scared?

2

Reuben poked his head out of the door and swiveled it to the left, then to the right. He paused and listened for a minute, to ensure that he was alone.

Mama and Daddy's master suite was at the opposite end of the house, but he wouldn't be surprised to find one or both of them lurking near his childhood bedroom. Whenever he visited, they hovered like moths attracted to a flame, or parents afraid to let their active toddler out of sight. This afternoon, he felt like a teenager about to sneak a call to a girl for whom they didn't care.

In reality, he just needed to talk privately with his wife. He had made a big decision today, and he wanted Peyton's assurance that she was still on board.

One minute he was jazzed about returning to Jubilant, and the next, he wondered whether he had lost his mind. He had a great job at Amazon.com; he and his wife owned a nice home; and Peyton's parents lived half an hour away and helped with Charles David whenever they needed. Was he really going to uproot his family from all they knew and loved in Seattle, and move them to the Texas town he hadn't considered home since he left for college?

Reuben sat on the edge of the twin bed positioned against the wall and marveled at how small and confining this space now felt, given that he had once considered this room his haven. Then again, by the time he left for college, he had become almost claustrophobic—anxious to free himself from this house, the family's façade of normalcy, and memories that had begun to suffocate him.

Peyton had always been supportive, but he wasn't sure how she would take the news that the big changes they'd been mulling over for months were really going to happen. He had accepted the job offer, and in four weeks, Jubilant would be their home. He could hardly believe it; how could he expect her to?

Reuben pulled his BlackBerry from its hip holster and hit the speed dial code for their home phone number.

He smiled when she picked up on the third ring and greeted him in typical singsong fashion. "Hello, baby!"

"Hey, Peyt," he said. He imagined her sitting on the floor of their family room, playing a card game with Charles David or cheering him on as he enjoyed his favorite race car video game on the Wii, and his voice grew husky. "Well, it's official."

"Really? He accepted your counteroffer?"

"Yep."

The long seconds of silence before she spoke again told him she was stunned. "You're really moving me away from my family, all the way to the other side of the country?"

Now he paused. He closed his eyes and took a deep breath. He was asking a lot. A whole lot. But he had to give this a try. "Not the entire other side. We're not moving to the East Coast," he said and chuckled. "But the South is very different from what you're used to. You still okay with this?"

"Yeah, babe," Peyton said. "It will be an adjustment, but once I learn my way around, I'll be okay. And Charles David will be fine."

"You sure?"

"As long as we're with you, and you're happy, I'm sure, Reuben. You need to do this. We'll be fine. Just get me a cell phone with a good roaming plan. You know I need to talk to Mom every day."

"It's a deal . . ."

"Why do you sound hesitant instead of excited?"

She knew him so well. He wanted to talk to her about it, but working through what was fueling his jitters might take all night. Mama and Daddy's over-exuberance about his decision to come home, coupled with his own ambivalence about whether that's what he really should be doing, had unnerved him.

He had run from his demons long enough, though, and this move would allow Charles David to get to know the rest of his family. Reuben needed more quality time to get to know them again too. His number one reason for making this move was to reconnect with his sisters, although at the moment, he didn't think his presence would make much difference to Indigo or Yasmin. Reuben hadn't been fooled this afternoon at lunch; he had recognized the anger and frustration behind Indigo's tears.

"I'm okay, Peyt," Reuben finally said. He ran his muscular hand over his low-cut hair and settled back on the bed. At six feet three, his feet dangled over the edge.

"I guess I'm adjusting to the idea of this big move myself, that's all. But it's the right decision. Has to be. Otherwise, there's no chance of me ever moving forward."

Peyton sighed, and Reuben imagined that she was cradling the phone, wishing she could hug him. She always held him close when he talked about his biological parents and how they died.

"Remember what my father told you when you discussed this move with him, Reuben? I agree with him—you may never get over the deaths of Mom Meredith or Dad David, but you do need to get on with life. If this is the next step toward healing, let's take it."

Reuben smiled. He loved his little brown-skinned doll. Nothing seemed to rattle her.

Mama and Daddy, Indigo and Yasmin, and their extended family had gotten to know Peyton when she visited Jubilant with him three or four times in recent years, and they marveled at her sweet spirit and determination. But they didn't know that she also was a lot of fun and unafraid of risks—some of the very qualities he needed more of.

They were going to fall in love with her in no time, just like he had. What worried Reuben most now was whether anyone other than Mama and Daddy could love him again.

3

Reuben stood in the center of the dining room, squirming like an awkward teenager put on display for his parents' friends.

Mama's effusive praise made him want to hitchhike to Washington State. She had been chattering nonstop about his new job in the Jubilant mayor's office since Aunt Melba arrived an hour ago. When Rachelle and Gabe walked in, she shared the details again.

Mama had insisted on the last-minute gathering after deciding that Reuben's news was worth celebrating.

"Mayor Henning met Reuben at Melba's Christmas party last December and was really impressed," Mama said. This time she was telling the story to Indigo's fiancé, Max. He had arrived separately from Indigo a few minutes earlier, after wrapping up a photo shoot at a downtown business function.

Reuben fixed his smile. Didn't Mama remember that Max had attended that party too and had witnessed the connection between the two men?

"Reuben told the mayor that he might want to move back to Jubilant, and they began talking privately about Reuben joining his team," she said. "Mayor Henning created this new position based on Reuben's skill set. Basically, Reuben will be getting all of the city's computer systems updated, right, son?"

Mama raised a questioning eyebrow while everyone turned to listen. If he weren't so tense, Reuben would have laughed at her attempts to describe his new job in layman's terms.

"That's about right. I'll be overseeing an upgrade of the computers in City Hall and then getting the system there to 'talk' to the computer systems in other city agencies, so that there's more efficient functioning across the board. It's almost like building a new bridge but still using the old bridge until the new one is ready. For a while, you have two bridges standing side by side. When the new one is sturdy enough, you have to build an off ramp from the old one onto the new one, without people noticing much difference in their efforts to cross from one side to the other.

"After that project's finished, I'll draft a strategic plan for revamping internal communications for city employees and improving citizens' access to online services and products."

Aunt Melba leaned toward Reuben and hugged his neck.

"Congratulations, nephew," she said. "Sounds like an important job, but it's not quite as exciting as working for Amazon.com is it? You sure you're ready for small-town life again?"

Mama glared at her sister. "Of course he is, Melba. Besides, what's more important than being with your family?"

Mama approached Reuben and steered him to a chair on the left side of the long, cherry table. "Sit here, between your sisters."

She motioned for Indigo and Yasmin to fill the seats that flanked him. Yasmin rolled her eyes and trudged to her designated spot.

Indigo leaned against the cherrywood buffet and folded her arms. She remained expressionless, but Reuben knew an attitude when he saw one. Max pulled Indigo toward the table and led her to the chair on Reuben's right. He sat on the other side of Indigo and continued to hold her hand under the table.

Now that Mama had everyone positioned where she wished—her three children and Max on one side of the table and her sister Melba, niece Rachelle, and Rachelle's husband Gabe on the other—she beamed.

"Wait until I tell your uncle Herbert." Mama glanced at Rachelle. "You haven't called your father, have you? I want to be the first to let my brother know that my baby's moving back home."

Reuben saw Gabe nudge Rachelle with his elbow.

"I wouldn't dare steal your thunder, Aunt Irene," Rachelle said, struggling to keep from laughing. "I know how excited you are."

"Everybody does!" Indigo said in a lighthearted tone accompanied by a wide, plastic smile.

Reuben hadn't spent much time with her during his return trips over the past four years, despite his efforts, but he knew Indigo well enough now to recognize the frustration that had reared its head earlier in the day, during lunch.

He leaned toward her, prepared to call her on it. But Aunt Melba chimed in first, with a raised eyebrow.

"Yes, Indigo, you're right. Your mama is excited and so is the rest of the family. We can't wait for Reuben to move back with Peyton and David."

Reuben didn't correct her. He and Peyton had called their son by both his first and middle names since Charles David was a baby, because he liked one name better and Peyton preferred the other. It had become second nature to them and to Peyton's family, who lived on the outskirts of Seattle and saw the boy often. But Reuben's relatives typically used David, despite Reuben and Peyton's repeated reminders. Reuben had finally given up, assuming that they preferred to use "David" because that was his biological father's name, and because Daddy (his grandfather) was also named Charles.

"We've missed having you around on a regular basis for a long time, Reuben, and it will be nice to have a young child to love on," Aunt Melba said. "It's a blessing when you can still come home and find your family intact. And it's a blessing when that family welcomes you with open arms. That's what we're doing."

Aunt Melba winked at Reuben, then extended her arms to grasp hands with Rachelle right next to her and Yasmin across the table. "Want to bless the food, since your dad isn't joining us for dinner tonight?"

Reuben held his breath when all eyes fell on him. The grace he usually said with his son—"Good food, good meat, good God, let's eat!"—would not go over well with this group.

He noticed a hint of a smile on Indigo's face. She wanted to see him squirm, and she was having her way.

He coughed.

Max leaned past Indigo and grinned at him. "Mind if I say grace in your honor tonight, man?"

Reuben could have kissed the brother. "Go for it."

Everyone clasped hands and bowed their heads. Indigo held his hand loosely and Reuben's heart constricted. He got the message: she might be forced to be in his presence, but she was going to use every chance she got to let him know she wasn't enjoying it.

When dinner was served, his sister kept her eyes on the roast, garlic mashed potatoes, corn, and greens that Mama had whipped up in just hours. He usually wolfed down the traditional southern fare, but tonight, not even the hot buttered rolls could take his mind off of his nagging fears.

He wanted to pick a fight, to get whatever was bothering Indigo out in the open. But they weren't kids anymore; there was no guarantee that pushing her buttons would yield the results he longed for—reconciliation, love, and friendship.

He'd been trying to figure out for months how to crumble her wall of resentment. Nothing had worked, and Mama's excessive joy tonight was only making things worse.

Reuben decided to change the subject, hoping that for once, it might penetrate her shell. "How are the wedding plans coming?" he asked.

Indigo shrugged and took another bite of food. Reuben took the cue and decided to leave her alone. He turned toward his baby sister.

"What's new with you, Miss Yasmin?"

The teenager mimicked her sister's nonchalance. "The same ol' same ol'."

He must have lived in Seattle too long—this chick was talking in code. "Excuse me?"

Yasmin sighed. "I keep forgetting you're *thirty-one*. Let me translate: The same old, same old stuff. Nothing's going on since Mama and Daddy decided that they still want me to be their baby and stay under their thumbs. I'll start my senior year of high school in three weeks, but in the meantime, I'm just watching summer wind down. I helped Aunt Melba at the hair salon today and came home to hear your *wonderful* news."

Reuben sat back and folded his arms.

"Yasmin, that was out of line." Cousin Rachelle laid down her fork and frowned in surprise.

Yasmin smirked, seemingly at no one in particular, and took a long sip of sweet tea before responding to Rachelle. "The truth will set you free."

Reuben peeked at Mama and awaited her response. Neither

Mama nor Daddy tolerated disrespect. He remembered receiving threats of a spanking at seventeen.

But Daddy was in bed this evening, resting and trying to get his blood pressure down. And Mama was intent on doting on her son/grandson, oblivious to the blanket of tension her praise was knitting. She took a bite of her potatoes and kept her head lowered.

Rachelle's eyes blazed. Gabe elbowed her in the side again. He looked at Reuben and reassured him with a smile.

"Man, now that you're leaving Amazon, does this mean no more free shipping? No more free gifts? Think about your cousins! You sure you want to give up that great job to move to Jubilant?"

This time Rachelle elbowed him.

"*You* moved here from Houston to practice small-town medicine, doc," Reuben said. "What's the problem?"

Both men laughed. Reuben was grateful for the camaraderie.

"It'll be good for Charles David to have family close by," Reuben said. "He's at the age where he's asking more questions about where I grew up and what you guys are like. Plus, if we're going to leave a place as familiar to Peyton as Seattle, she could use some extra help every so often."

Rachelle nodded, and Reuben remembered her offer to ask her daughter Taryn, who at a year older than Yasmin was already in college, if she'd be interested in a part-time babysitting job when Peyton and Charles David arrived.

"Taryn loves kids. I think I told you that she volunteers in the nursery at church. She said she can help you guys out some once you get settled, and there's no need to pay her. She's only taking fifteen hours in the fall, because she'll be a cheerleader this year."

Reuben grinned. "Your baby is an Everson College Egyptian? My, my, my. I remember when I used to go to games just to watch the halftime performances with the dancers and cheerleaders . . ."

"My goodness," Indigo said sweetly. "As long as you've been gone, it's funny that you remember anything about this place."

Reuben turned toward her. "Indie, let's talk—"

Mama jumped to her feet. "Let's have dessert. I made a German chocolate cake and a peach cobbler. Indigo, can you get them for me, from the kitchen?"

Reuben sucked his teeth.

The pinched smile plastered on Mama's face couldn't mask the fear in her eyes. She saw this family feud brewing, and she was doing her best to halt it. But sooner or later he and his sister were going to have it out.

Just because he'd been gone for a while, living life on his terms, didn't mean he couldn't ever come home. He had a right to be a part of this family as much as she did. If his presence was bugging her, she'd better grow up and get over it.

In thirty days he was returning with his wife and son, ready to join the mayor's staff and become part of the fabric of Jubilant. Indigo wasn't going to make him regret this move. Too much was at stake.

4

"It takes a lot of energy to stay mad at someone, girlfriend."

Indigo had an angry retort ready, but knew better than to utter it. Had Rachelle been talking to her friend Shelby? Or to Max? Regardless, Indigo knew her favorite cousin was right: nursing her animosity for Reuben was distracting and draining.

She couldn't help it, though.

"He can do whatever he wants, without being called on it," Indigo said. "Go off to college and return a decade later—no questions asked. Uproot his family from his wife's hometown and return here as some kind of hero—no explanations necessary."

Indigo chucked the silverware from the evening meal into the dishwasher while Rachelle stood next to her, scrubbing Mama's large pots and pans. Indigo thought about the advice she still needed from Mama but hadn't had a chance to pursue.

"Everything is 'Reuben this' and 'Reuben that'! He's coming home—great. But does that mean the rest of us don't matter?"

Aunt Melba paused from tucking a covered dish in the fridge and turned toward Indigo. She put a hand on her curvy hip. "Indigo, are you sixteen or twenty-six?"

Indigo stole a glance at the door leading from the kitchen into the hallway. As defiant as she felt, she would be ashamed if Mama walked in and overheard this conversation. Strains of dialogue from Mama's favorite syndicated TV western, *The Lone Ranger*, wafted from the family room. With the masked ranger and Tonto entertaining her, Indigo knew Mama was oblivious to the banter—soon to be lecture, it seemed—taking place in the kitchen.

Indigo sighed and plopped into a chair at the oblong kitchen table. She was near tears. "I know I'm acting childish," she finally said.

"And selfish?" Aunt Melba asked.

That diagnosis stung. "Why do you say that?"

Aunt Melba and Rachelle joined her at the table.

Rachelle reached for her hand. "Indie, you're the one who convinced Reuben to attend the family barbecue for the first time in years, just before you left for grad school. Didn't you want him to come back home, to be part of the family?"

Indigo nodded and let the tears fall.

She peered this time toward the door leading outside, to the patio and backyard, where Reuben had joined Max and Gabe for a game of basketball. If any of them walked in right now, she'd be mortified.

"I thought that's what I wanted. He's my only brother, and his absence left a big hole in Mama and Daddy's hearts. I just wanted them to be happy, to heal. Yasmin didn't remember much about him because she was only six when he went off to college. But I missed him, and I was hurt when he never really came back. He called and wrote to me sometimes, but he was never part of the family again. I thought his coming back four years ago would make us whole again. Hasn't happened."

Aunt Melba reared back in the chair and folded her arms. "Go on."

Indigo wiped her wet cheeks with her thumbs and shook her head.

"What more can I say? I don't know why I'm tripping. I wanted him to be part of the family, but I guess I feel like it's been too easy. No one has bothered to ask him why he left in the first place. And he's never apologized or even explained his long absence. It hurt, Aunt Melba. I just feel like he breezed out and breezed back in and gets the royal treatment regardless of how much pain his estrangement caused us."

Aunt Melba smiled. "Now we're getting somewhere. Keep talking."

Indigo frowned. She didn't know how to explain herself without sounding more juvenile than they had already accused her of being. She felt like a volcano, and what was erupting left her vulnerable. "It was fine for us all to be wrapped up in 'Reubenmania' when he first returned, but Mama and Daddy still haven't come back to earth. I'm planning my wedding—that's a big deal to me—and I can only get Mama's halfhearted attention because she caters to Reuben's every whim. If he calls, she'll get off the phone with me or send me to the family room with Yasmin. If he's in town, our scheduled plans get postponed. That happened today—I asked her to meet me for lunch so we could discuss something important, but he came with her, and I'm still not any clearer about the choices I need to make. I'm just not ready for more of that when he moves here.

"If it's not Reuben, she'll make it her business to entertain little Charles David and help Peyton adjust to her new surroundings. That's all good, but I still need her too. Is that selfish?"

Rachelle and Melba looked at each and burst into laughter.

A fresh lump formed in Indigo's throat. They'd never made light of her feelings before.

When Rachelle had composed herself, she reached for Indigo's hand again.

"I'm sorry, Indie," she said between breaths. "We're not laughing at your concerns. That 'Reubenmania' thing got us. Where on earth did that come from?"

She laughed again, and this time, Indigo chuckled. She hadn't meant to reveal the secret terminology.

"That's what Shelby and I coined the . . . the *hysteria* Mama and Daddy seem to find themselves in whenever it comes to their son."

"That's a good one," Aunt Melba said and grinned. "We'll keep it to ourselves. Back to the issue at hand, though. Your feelings are a bit selfish, but—" she raised her palm to silence Indigo's protest, "—they are understood. Your wedding is a big deal. You deserve to have extra-special support and attention during this time. And I agree, Irene and Charles have been swooning over Reuben since he came back into the fold. But they'll get over it. They're just trying to reassure themselves that he's here to stay this time, and I think his move back to Jubilant will help."

Indigo hugged herself. "I don't know if it will help or make things worse."

"Want me to talk to her about how you're feeling?" Aunt Melba asked. "Have you even tried to talk to her?"

"No," Indigo said. "I haven't wanted to make her feel like she has to hide her joy. Mama deserves to be happy. It's just hard for me not to feel like it's at my expense, and even Yasmin's."

"Well, I'm happy to say something subtle to her," Melba offered again.

Indigo didn't know how "subtle" her aunt's subtle would be: Melba wasn't known for mincing words.

"Is Yasmin feeling this way too?" Aunt Melba asked.

Rachelle pushed her seat back from the table and resumed washing dishes. "I don't know what Yasmin's issue is, but that girl is worrying me," she said. "She's got a big chip on her shoulder, and she's even stopped coming to the church youth group meetings."

Indigo nodded, thankful that the focus had shifted to someone else. She wasn't sure whether Aunt Melba would say something to Mama, but she would leave that between them.

Rachelle was right, though—her baby sister seemed to be spiraling downward.

"Mama says none of Yasmin's old friends, the girls she used to hang out with at St. Peter's, call anymore," Indigo said. "And she's been caught sneaking out of the house twice. Does Taryn have any idea what's going on?"

Rachelle squeezed the water from her sudsy sponge and attacked another pot that had been soaking in the sink. "Taryn stays really busy these days with the girlfriends she made in her freshman dorm. She and Yasmin still talk, but they're not as close as they once were. Taryn says Yasmin is still angry that Aunt Irene and Uncle Charles made her stop modeling two years ago."

Aunt Melba placed her palms on the table and pushed herself up from her seat. "These knees are getting creaky! I've started water aerobics to keep this body in shape, because walking on the treadmill was getting painful."

Indigo marveled at how Aunt Melba, now in her early seventies, still looked a decade younger and had the curves that women half her age would kill for. Even after a stroke and now problems with her knees, she had a beauty, magnetic personality, and straightforward wit that drew others to her. Mama's side of the family definitely had good genes. She hoped they would help preserve her too.

When Melba reached the sink, she took the pots and pans Rachelle had washed and dried and tucked them under the granite-topped island that served as the centerpiece of the kitchen.

"Yasmin has been angry about the modeling situation for way too long." Aunt Melba straightened after sliding the last pan into place. "I understand that that's her dream, but if that's what God intends for her to do, he'll bring her back to it."

"Oh really. When? How?"

Indigo, Rachelle, and Aunt Melba turned to find a defiant Yasmin leaning her lanky frame against the doorway and scowling.

"None of you seem to realize how the modeling industry either embraces you or spits you out. At seventeen I'm in my prime. I should be on runways in Paris and participating in fashion shoots in New York. But Mama and Daddy want to keep me sheltered. They don't want to let go of their baby." She walked over to the table, plopped in a seat, and laid her head down. "Maybe now that Reuben's family is coming, they won't miss me if I leave."

Indigo raised an eyebrow at Yasmin, but for the first time recognized the unflattering truth about herself. Aunt Melba and Rachelle were right—all of her whining and pouting over Reuben made her sound like a petulant teenager. Not pretty. She needed to get it together.

"Yasmin, what's that supposed to mean?" Indigo asked. "Don't act like you don't remember. Mama and Daddy pulled you out of your modeling contract because your roommate for one of the Dallas jobs got caught with cocaine, and because another model you befriended began struggling with bulimia. They were scared that you would start making yourself throw up again.

"What should they have done, Yas? Let you go down the tubes with those folks? If the pressure was causing those girls to suffer, why wouldn't it affect you too? I think they did the right thing."

Yasmin glared at Indigo. "I wasn't Meghan or Lila. I had already been treated for bulimia, and I loved my job. You think I would have messed that up by doing something stupid? Think about it—I worked for Ford Models! Mama and Daddy had no right to kill my career."

Indigo shook her head. "Yas, you're so young. It's too early to call anything in your life 'dead.' Another opportunity will come around when the time is right."

Aunt Melba walked over to Yasmin and stroked the girl's long black hair, which was streaked with burgundy and blonde highlights. "Who's going to hire you with this punk rock look, anyway? Since when did you find this style becoming?"

Yasmin sighed. Indigo knew the answer her sister wouldn't dare share: Yas's new friends had encouraged it. It looked awful, but it matched the girl's attitude.

Rachelle dried the last dish, folded the dishtowel, and laid it on the island. "I want to go back to what Yasmin said a few minutes ago, about Reuben. Sounds like you have the same concerns as Indigo about his return. What gives?"

Yasmin pursed her lips. "I knew I shouldn't have come in here when I heard the three of you talking. We're not at the salon. I'm not up for a 'Pour-out-your-heart, ladies only' session right now."

Indigo, Rachelle, and Aunt Melba didn't budge.

"What do you want me to say?" Yasmin finally responded. "Reuben's alright. He's my brother and all, and I guess I love him. But I really don't know him. All I know is that he can do no wrong, at least in Mama and Daddy's eyes. I can't go out with my friends, model, or skip church or the youth group meeting without getting grief, but if he sneezes the wrong way, Mama and Daddy declare it marvelous." Yasmin leaned back and crossed her arms.

"We'll see what happens. But until Reuben gives me a reason to personally be excited about his return home, I'll keep wondering, what's the big deal."

Indigo again heard an infantile version of her own complaints in her sister's response and acknowledged the truth about herself—she was both jealous and selfish. But it sounded like it wouldn't matter. Mama and Daddy were going to lavish an extraordinary amount of love on Reuben and his family no matter what. Even Yasmin saw that.

"Your brother's return is a big deal, you two," Aunt Melba said. "It just is. And since we're all family, we're going to find a way to celebrate him and be sincere about it." She looked at Yasmin. "I'm not getting in the middle of your parents' decision about your modeling career, Yasmin. You have to trust that they had your best interest at heart. But until you stop whining about it and acting bitter, you're going to kill a lot more of the dreams that are within your reach. You can't recognize new opportunities when you're stuck on what happened in the past."

Then Melba turned toward Indigo. "I'll talk to Irene about all of this whenever the time seems right. In the meantime, looks like Rachelle and I'll have to get busy helping you finalize everything for the wedding."

Indigo smiled, but her heart was still sad.

These two ladies were more than just a cousin and aunt. They were like another pair of mothers. But they still didn't replace Mama. Mama had been there when she had picked out the dress she intended to wear when she was engaged to marry Brian. Mama stood by her when she had ended that relationship and had cried with her when she called to tell her that she had fallen in love with Max. When Max proposed a year later, they had celebrated together.

Indigo was grateful for Aunt Melba's and Rachelle's loyalty and support; but before she became someone's wife, she prayed that she could share this special time with the woman who had raised her, without the thought of, or the needs of, Reuben lurking in the shadows.

5

Max and Indigo strolled to her car, parked in front of her parents' house, with their arms around each other's waist.

When they reached her Jetta, Max leaned against the driver's side door and pulled Indigo toward him. He enveloped her in a hug and leaned his head toward her for a kiss. Despite the veil of darkness, she saw the tenderness in his eyes and melted. She could stay like this all night. For the first time today, everything felt right in her world.

"You okay?" he asked, just above a whisper.

Indigo nodded and smiled. "Yeah, I'm okay. Did I show out too much at dinner tonight?"

"Yes, you did. But I still love you."

Indigo loved the fact that he was honest with her, no matter what. No secrets, no sugarcoating reality; just the truth, from the heart.

"I'm glad," she said and sighed. She laid her head on his muscular chest and hugged him tighter, knowing what would come next.

Max had to be curious about whether she'd reached a decision on his offers. She hadn't, though, because she knew she was too close to the situation. She wanted some objective feedback from Mama.

If that wasn't going to happen, maybe she should just talk to Rachelle and Aunt Melba, and rely on Shelby to share her perspective as a fairly new wife.

"Want me to follow you home so we can talk or watch a movie?" he asked. It was Friday night, and if they hadn't been arm-twisted into dinner by Mama, they would have gotten together anyway when he finished his photo shoot to grab a bite to eat and catch a movie.

It wasn't late by their standards—just 9:30 p.m. But Indigo felt drained. Plus, she didn't want to get into a deep discussion with him until she'd had some time to think about how she wanted to start her married life. Their wedding was just a few months away, so Max had every right to know how she was feeling about the suggestions he'd made for their business and personal lives. But she wasn't ready to give him answers. She still felt too uncertain about one of his requests.

She looked up at him and smiled.

"I think I'm going to pass tonight on hanging out, if you don't mind. Maybe I just need to go home and get in bed, so I can wake up with a new attitude."

Max peered at her and smirked. "You mean to tell me all the drama that happens every time your brother visits could be alleviated with an extra nap? Try again, babe. You just aren't ready to talk about our future, are you?"

She looked away, but Max gently grasped her chin and turned her head back toward him. He looked into her eyes and kissed her.

"You take some time for yourself tonight, Indie. I'll go by the studio and get caught up on some work. See you in the morning?"

She was embarrassed, yet grateful. "Thanks for being patient with me, Max. I love you, baby. See you in the morning—I'll cook you breakfast, okay?"

"Since I can't get any answers from you, at least have my pancakes, omelet, and bacon ready in the morning."

Indigo raised an eyebrow. "Watch it, brother. You're marrying Indigo Burns, not my mother, Irene. In a minute, I'm going to invite you over to cook for *me* while I sit and watch."

They both laughed. Max stepped away from the door and opened it so Indigo could slide into the driver's seat. He leaned down and kissed her again.

"Call me when you get home, okay? And try to take it easy—things with Reuben are going to work out. You may have to sit your parents down and tell them how you're feeling. You never know how that could help."

Indigo placed her hands on the steering wheel and shrugged. "I'll think about it," she said, doubting even as she spoke that Mama and Daddy would be willing, or able, to appreciate her concerns. She would be happy at this point to get them to talk to her about anything unrelated to her brother and his family.

Max closed Indigo's car door and trotted over to his SUV. He waved before jumping in and flicking on the headlights. Indigo started her car and followed him down the block and out of the subdivision. When they reached a main road, Max waved from his rearview mirror and turned right. Indigo waited for the traffic light to switch to green and turned left.

She lowered the radio volume as strains of Jazmine Sullivan's latest hit floated from the speakers, and sighed.

With or without getting others' opinions, she was going to have to talk with Max tomorrow about where they would live and how they would work.

Not only did Max want to buy a house together now, so they could move in right after the wedding, he also wanted her to become co-owner of his photography studio, before the ink dried on their wedding license. The thought of co-owning property and a business before she got used to saying her new last name rattled her.

Her heart told her yes—take this man, his offers, and run all the way to the altar. This time, she wasn't second-guessing herself. She had no doubts that Max Shepherd was her soul mate. They shared the same values as well as the same career, and he had a strong work ethic and commitment to serving others. He was thoughtful and generous, and he just happened to be fine. Her heart swelled with pride when she was with him, simply because he was a good man. With one look, or by uttering a syllable of her name, he grabbed her attention and caused her heart to beat faster.

Still, her practical side was wary of the red flags. Namely, whether it was wise for them to be together 24/7, no matter how much in love they were. She wondered if they would need time apart to keep from taking each other for granted, or simply to miss each other enough to look forward to reconnecting each evening.

She sighed and dialed Shelby's number. When she didn't get an answer, she glanced at the clock on her dashboard. Of course. It was 10 p.m. Shelby and Hunt were on a date of their own.

Indigo pulled into the parking space in front of her townhouse and grabbed her oversized leather purse from the driver's seat. She briskly walked the well-lit path to her front door and stepped inside.

She auto-dialed Max's number on her cell as she slid out of her shoes and picked them up to take them to her bedroom. "I'm here, babe," she said. "See you in the morning."

"Get some rest, okay? No fretting about Reuben and his crew."

Indigo laughed and flopped across her bed. "Yes sir. Love you."

She laid the phone beside her on the comforter and closed her eyes. Max was off track tonight. She was thinking about him right now, instead of her brother. His plan to sell his brick rancher so they could start off in a new home suited her fine. She hadn't been too keen on trying to remodel his bachelor pad anyway. But whether she should join him in work was the troubling question.

She stayed as she was, stretched out across her bed with her eyes closed, and mentally ran down the list of pros and cons about Max's offer. She started with the pros: since her move back to Jubilant from New York City a year ago, she had been able to use Max's studio to process photos she shot on the freelance jobs that took her all over the country and sometimes to other parts of the world. Max had been a professional photographer about five years longer than she. Operating a joint business would be efficient and could be marketed to raise both of their profiles; and Max was a good businessman. His plans were usually successful.

She rolled onto her side and grabbed a pillow to hug. Time to consider the potential cons: merging business and personal decisions could put a strain on their relationship if they didn't always see eye to eye. One of her goals was to try more creative projects and accept unusual business opportunities, while Max veered toward safe and steady clients, regardless of whether the assignments were exciting or fulfilling. And could they truly shut off work at the end of the day and make their home a haven?

The list of pros outnumbered the cons, but Indigo knew the two cons could cause serious issues. Would Mama urge her to dive in, or be cautious, even with a man she trusted completely?

Indigo had lived and traveled enough to know that anything worth having didn't have to be, and probably shouldn't be, rushed. Her experience with her former fiancé, Brian, and a few other disappointments, were tender proof.

She needed Mama's sound reasoning to balance her giddiness. Mama would tell her whether to follow her heart or check the emotions at the door. With Mama not available though, where should she turn? Indigo rolled onto her back and opened her eyes. Her gaze landed on her nightstand, on her Bible.

Why hadn't she thought to pray about this? The question came with a twinge of guilt, and she realized it was deserved. In all of her fussing and waiting on Mama, she hadn't done the one thing that she knew would be at the top of Mama's list of advice: pray about it.

Indigo stared at the ceiling and tried to find the words to talk to God about her concerns. Finally, she released what was filling her heart.

Tell me what to do about it, God. All of it. My life with Max. My feelings toward Reuben. My fears about the future. Tell me, and help me hear you.

She pushed herself up off the bed and headed to the bathroom to wash her face and brush her teeth, and unbidden, the kind of response Aunt Melba would give her came to mind. Or was it God?

Whatever the source, she realized that simply asking God for answers wasn't going to be enough. This "voice" cautioned her that whenever and however God replied, she would have to find the courage to act on what he said.

6

Peyton could call it "the favor of God" if she wanted. Whatever.

Reuben was simply thrilled that their 2,500 square-foot contemporary home had sold within seven days of being put on the market. Seattle routinely ranked as one of the best places to live, but a turnaround of that speed exceeded his expectations.

Now, three weeks later, Reuben and his family were settling into a spacious, single-floor, all-brick home twice the size of their place in Washington State. The cheaper cost of living had allowed them to purchase more house and land, and to afford upgrades and the special equipment they wanted to install to make the place as easy as possible for Peyton to become familiar with and call her own.

She maneuvered fairly well in most settings, but when your home could truly be your haven, all the better.

Reuben trotted down the three steps that led into the sunken family room and found Peyton counting her footsteps as she walked its perimeter. He let her finish before speaking.

"Have you decided where you want the sofa?"

Her luscious locks bobbed at her shoulders when she nodded. They framed her cocoa face perfectly and drew attention away from her unfocused eyes. She looked as adorable as she had the day Reuben had met her in downtown Seattle, trying to make it to jury duty on time.

He could pick her up now with little effort and just about carry her on his shoulders. But if he tried that while she was concentrating on positioning the furniture, she'd swat him.

"Let's put the sofa in front of the fireplace," Peyton finally said and pointed in the right direction. "I just counted off steps for the love seat, so it can go behind me, to the left of the sofa."

"What about my chair?"

"Will it work in that corner near the wall of windows, where we'll also have the bookcase?"

Reuben had been married to Peyton for six years and had dated her for a year before that, and it still amazed him how quickly she could orient herself to surroundings she couldn't see. Sighted people would have more trouble than this decorating a room; she breezed through it.

Before they moved in, Reuben hired contractors to outfit the house with surround sound features and computer technology that spoke to Peyton when she entered a room and helped her know whether the lights were on or off, or whether the oven temperature or thermostat were set correctly.

Otherwise, Peyton ruled the world with her cane, a keen sense of hearing, and a willingness to allow strangers to help her get where she was going. She'd had a guide dog as a teenager, but when Beau died suddenly from a heart murmur, she decided to pursue independence without the canine assistance. As her parents tell it, she never "looked" back.

Peyton's biggest issue here in Jubilant would be the lack of a convenient way to get around the city. The bus wasn't as popular a mode of transportation in a town this size, so she'd have to rely more on friends and family, or even taxi services or shuttles.

Reuben had added expenses in the family budget to cover the costs of whatever paid transportation Peyton settled on. He knew it wouldn't take her long to begin exploring. She would go stir crazy if she were housebound.

Charles David rounded a corner and leapt through the doorway. He paused when he saw Reuben and watched in fascination as Reuben shoved the brown leather recliner toward the corner Peyton had designated. The movers had plopped almost everything in the center of the room, since the Burnses hadn't decided on placement before they left. That meant Reuben had quite a bit of heavy lifting to do in this room and in the living room.

"Play Go Fish with me, Daddy!" Charles David giggled and tried to climb on Reuben's back.

"Not right now, little man," Reuben said and plopped into his chair. "I'm about to get up in a sec and help Mommy put the rest of the furniture in place. Have you found your other toys?"

Charles David scrambled onto Reuben's lap and pouted. "Moving is no fun. I can't find anything, and you and Mommy don't have time to play."

Peyton walked along the wall, touching it to guide her toward the door to the half bathroom adjacent to the family room. "Charles David, bring me the small trash can in the box by the door, okay? If you help Mommy finish getting everything right in the bathroom, I'll get my deck of Go Fish cards out of my purse and play one round with you."

Charles David jumped down from Reuben's lap and ran over to his mother. The sage green trash can she was referring to was sitting next to a big box, about half a foot away. "Got it, Mommy!" he yelled.

He handed it to Peyton, who felt her way into the bathroom and placed it adjacent to the sink.

"Good job, baby boy. My purse is on the table in the kitchen. Bring it here so I can find the cards."

When Charles David dashed away, Peyton made her way over to Reuben, this time counting the steps instead of clutching the wall. She climbed into his lap, where Charles David had been, and planted a kiss on his lips.

"Welcome to our great adventure, babe."

Reuben smiled and encircled her tiny waist with his arms. "Thanks for doing this, Peyt. I hope we'll be happy here."

She kissed him again. "I've prayed about it, Reuben. Everything will be fine. More than fine. We're going to thrive here. You just wait and see."

He had confessed his concerns about the cold shoulder his sisters were giving him, and Peyton had reassured him again just this morning that the issues were theirs—not his—to worry about.

Charles David reappeared, lugging Peyton's floppy flowered purse over his right shoulder. Peyton slid from Reuben's lap and found a spot on the floor where she could keep her promise to her son.

Reuben watched them play with her Braille set of cards and fumbled with his inner dialogue.

Please, God, if you're really there, do bless this move. Clear the cobwebs and make it alright. Especially with Indigo and Yasmin.

He must really be nervous. He had talked more to God in recent weeks than he had since . . . never mind that now. All he needed was for the prayer to work. If God didn't answer, this move just might be in vain.

7

What kind of photographer couldn't focus?

Indigo chided herself as she sat across the room from Max, watching him work on a spread for *Jubilant Today*, a glossy monthly magazine which regularly hired him to cover local social events.

She was supposed to be viewing frames of pictures she shot during a recent assignment for San Antonio's art museum, plus she needed to edit the images from a wedding that a friend of the family had convinced her to shoot last week. Instead, she kept picturing Max in the black tuxedo he had purchased for their special day.

Her friend Nizhoni, a former bridal consultant, had long ago landed a rewarding career as a flight attendant, but she was using her wedding expertise to help Indigo finalize details and look her best. Nizhoni had spotted the tuxes for Max and his groomsmen in a bridal magazine and had helped Indigo get a sample flown into the local bridal shop where she had once worked, for Max to try.

Max wasn't superstitious; he had insisted that Indigo join him for the fitting this afternoon to see if she liked how he looked in it. That was why she couldn't concentrate now. The wedding was in November, but she had wanted to marry him on the spot.

She pushed her chair back from her computer and rolled over to his station to plant a kiss on his cheek. Max kept his eyes on his computer screen and grinned.

"You haven't given me an answer yet, but I think I may take back the offer to make you a co-owner of this place, Miss Indigo."

Indigo sat back, surprised. "Oh really?"

Max still didn't look her way. "Look at you! You're harassing me while I'm trying to work. Now if I do what I feel like doing—turning off this computer and taking you home—we'd both miss our deadlines and be broke."

"We'd also be sinning, brotherman," Indigo said and swatted his shoulder. "I just gave you a kiss. How did you make that leap?"

This time he did look at her, and into her eyes. "The wedding is ninety-six days and eighteen hours away. How's that for making a leap?"

Indigo's heart danced. Max was something else. Waiting was a challenge for her too, but she knew it would be worth it.

She rolled the chair back to her computer to give both of them some breathing space. "So now you think we shouldn't go into business together, huh?"

Max paused and winked at her. "I was just teasing, girl. You're an ace photographer, and we make a great team. But you're also hard to resist. Maybe your first inclination is right: let's keep doing what we're doing—handling our clients separately—for a while, until we get settled into being Mr. and Mrs. Shepherd. One thing at a time, okay?"

Indigo nodded and smiled at him. "Gotcha."

Inwardly, she jumped for joy. Her instincts had been right: pray for God to work it out and let Max have the final say. In the end,

Max's decision had mirrored what she'd felt was right all along, and she hadn't had to make a big deal about it.

"Whatever you say, my king."

This time he rolled over to her and pulled her chair away from the computer so he could embrace her. He kissed her tenderly and smiled. "Are you going to be this agreeable after I put that ring on your finger?"

Indigo shrugged. "You'll have to wait and see. But I'm guessing if the king continues to treat the queen 'queenly' he won't have any problems during his reign."

"Cut out all that gibberish," he said and laughed.

Indigo looked into his eyes, thrilled to see a happiness and tenderness there that she thought she'd never experience again after her breakup with Brian. She and Brian had reached the conclusion individually and together that they couldn't and shouldn't wed, but getting over him hadn't been easy. Even if he didn't excite her, he was her first love, and she eventually accepted that she would always care for him.

Max had been her friend, but he pursued her with a patient, respectful determination. She had fallen in love with his kind heart and gentlemanly ways, yet she appreciated the fun-loving and sometimes silly sides that occasionally emerged. She was thankful that his whole heart belonged to her, without the trepidation she had eventually recognized in herself and in Brian during their last few weeks as a couple.

Seeing Max in that tux today nearly brought her to tears. What if she had forced another relationship before giving this man a chance? She would have missed out on the wonder of this journey with him.

He snapped her back to reality when he stroked her cheek and cleared his throat. "I know we've got to get back to work—my pages are due to the magazine first thing in the morning. But I have something to tell you, and I need to go ahead and get it off my chest."

Indigo's stomach flip-flopped. He'd just tried on the tux; surely she wasn't about to be jilted again. She sat back in her chair and tried to remain expressionless.

Max knew her well though; he reached over and grabbed her hand. "Don't even think the worst, babe. You know you've got my heart. But we've always promised to be honest and up-front about everything, so I need to tell you this now, before the day is over."

Indigo managed to squeak out a reply. "Go ahead then."

"I went down to City Hall this morning to drop off some aerial shots of the city at the urban planning office, and I ran into Reuben. We wound up having coffee, and we got to talking about the wedding. He's really happy for us, you know?"

Indigo held her breath and waited.

"He asked quite a few of the big brother questions—How am I going to take care of you? Am I prepared to be a good husband, and all of that. You would have been proud."

Would I really? Indigo mused. She couldn't believe it. Max was being sucked into Reubenmania.

He sighed. "Anyway, here's the deal: we had such a good talk, and I could tell that he really cares about you, and you know I've been trying to decide on a fourth groomsman. So before we parted this morning, I asked Reuben to stand up for me. He said yes."

What the—?

Indigo rolled her chair backward and took a few deep breaths to keep from saying something she might regret.

They had gone for a tux fitting, had a late lunch, and spent the afternoon working together, and he just now happened to remember that he invited the brother she was struggling to accept to be in their wedding party?

"Max, stop being funny."

"Indie, I'm not. I asked Reuben to be a groomsman. I think it will help bring us all closer."

Indigo stood up and grabbed her purse. She stared at Max and willed herself to calm down. "You know what I think? You need to decide whom you really want to be close to."

She strode toward the door without looking back.

"What about your deadline?" Max called after her.

Darn. She had to meet it. She would be back, but right now, she needed some space. Reuben was crowding every corner of her life, and even if she were being selfish or childish, her feelings mattered. Her concerns about her own wedding shouldn't be dismissed.

She had to get past this, though. Reuben clearly wasn't going anywhere anytime soon. Right now, she was going to take a walk. She would edit her pictures in another hour. Maybe Max would have cleared out by then.

8

For the first time in weeks, Reuben felt hopeful.

His unexpected meeting with Max this morning had given the two men a chance to get to know each other. Although Max, an Everson College graduate, was from New Jersey, both men had graduated from high school the same year and both had played college basketball.

Reuben was also struck by how much Max, with his mop of curly hair that he wore closely cropped these days, and his café au lait complexion, resembled Dad David—Indigo and Reuben's biological father, who had perished in the car crash with Mom Meredith.

Reuben knew Max had heard the details—from Indigo's perspective—but he explained anyway how he had been twelve, Indigo seven, and Yasmin just eight months old when their parents died. Mama and Daddy, their paternal grandparents, had kept photos of their biological mother and father throughout the house, to remind each of them of their parents, and not long after, Mama and Daddy had suggested a special name for the couple.

"We're going to raise you now, and we're going to love you like your parents did, so call us Mama and Daddy," Daddy had instructed Reuben and Indigo. "But don't ever feel like you have to forget my son and your mother—none of us ever will. They'll always be your parents. Let's come up with a comfortable name to call them when we talk about them, okay?"

Indigo had suggested Dad David and Mom Meredith, and the names had stuck.

With his toffee complexion, angular face, and thin, but muscular bone structure, Reuben was the spitting image of his father, which meant that Indigo was marrying someone who resembled all of the men already in her life.

Reuben had felt comfortable enough today to pepper Max with questions about how he had come to know and love Indigo, and why he felt he was ready for marriage.

"I probably started falling in love with her the first time I formally met her, at Hair Pizzazz, your aunt Melba's hair salon," Max told him. "I had been assigned by the *Jubilant Herald* to shoot Indigo's photo, because she had won an *O Magazine* photo contest. Just talking to her that brief time and seeing how beautiful she was, inside and out, left me intrigued. But Indie was engaged to Brian, so I tried to steer clear.

"When they broke up, she wouldn't let me get close, even though I could tell she might be interested. Since I had received my master's in digital photography from the same grad school in New York that she was attending, I volunteered my services a lot over the next two years. Those flights from Jubilant to New York City weren't cheap!" Max's laughter bellowed throughout the city hall coffee shop. "But the volunteer sessions gave me a good 'excuse' to be in New York at least once every six weeks to invite her out for coffee, then to a show, and eventually to dinner. She dated a few other guys off and on, but just before she graduated, we seemed to settle into a routine. I would travel to New York a few weekends a month, when I didn't have to be away on a photo gig, and at least once a month she would come home to Jubilant. It just seemed real, and right. I think we both knew we wanted to be together before we made it official."

Reuben listened and nodded. His and Peyton's relationship had unfolded in a very different fashion, but it sounded like there had been a similar chemistry, which eventually turned into adoration. They weren't fairytale romances, per se. Instead, the things that made their relationships beautiful were the steadfastness of their love, and a sincere interest in wanting the best for the other person, regardless of whether they were going to be together.

Max didn't say all of that, but Reuben felt it and saw it in his eyes. This man was a good brother, and he was going to be good to Indigo.

Still, Reuben was stunned when, just before they departed, Max grabbed him by the shoulder and asked him to be one of his groomsmen.

"In *your* wedding?"

Reuben was certain he had heard wrong. Max had to be in tune with Indigo's feelings; he had to know how Indigo felt about her brother. But Max had insisted.

"Indigo's going to be fine," Max said. "Before the wedding rolls around, you two can make a point of spending more time together and talking through whatever awkward issues you need to resolve. Maybe this invitation is just what you need to jumpstart a reconnection between you two."

"How can you be so sure?"

Max smiled. "Indigo can be stubborn—I mean, come on—your parents treated her like a princess from the time they took custody of you three. But she's a beautiful person. She's just wrestling with a few things right now, and she's still got some growing up to do. She'll work through it. Don't worry."

Reuben had been tempted to tell Max about the issues he was struggling with too, but thought better of it. They had hit it off, but their connection was still through Indigo. He wasn't sure yet whether he could trust Max to keep his confidences, and he wasn't ready just yet for Indigo to know the primary reason he'd felt led to move back to Jubilant. If he and his sisters were going to love each other and celebrate each other as siblings, he didn't want it to be forced, or out of guilt.

Reuben wondered this evening how she had reacted to Max's decision to include him in the wedding party. He wouldn't be surprised if Miss Indigo picked up the phone and called on Max's behalf to revoke the invitation. She had never been that over the top, but then again, he hadn't invaded her territory before.

Reuben and Max had traded cell phone numbers before going their separate ways this morning, with promises to get together soon for a game of basketball or golf. He was tempted to call Max now for an update on Indigo's response.

Instead, Reuben steered his SUV out of the downtown parking deck and headed home. His thoughts remained on Indigo, though, and how since his family's relocation, she had avoided spending any time with Peyton and Charles David. It ticked him off, but Peyton didn't seem to mind.

"She'll come around," Peyton said. "Don't force it. I'm sure it would help, though, if you told her about your dreams, or at least about the promise you want to honor. You can't keep holding all of this pain inside, Reuben."

Reuben trusted his wife's wisdom, because usually she was right, even when he didn't want her to be. But he wasn't ready to give a tell-all confession. He wanted Indigo and Yasmin to accept him just because, without feeling obligated. Then he'd tell them the full truth about his reasons for returning home.

For now, he had to cherish small successes. At least the nightmares had lessened in frequency since the move, and he didn't constantly feel like he was suffocating. He hadn't suffered any more panic attacks, either. Life was getting better. Plus, there was a strong possibility that he was going to be an important part of Indigo's special day. If she allowed him to stand with other members of her wedding party, he knew Mom Meredith would be smiling down on him and resting in peace.

9

Indigo and Max agreed via text to spend Sunday together.

Max sent the first message:

> R we going 2 church 2gether? Still
> having dinner at your parents'?

Indigo's response had been curt.

> Pick me up @10:30.

She had disregarded the peace offering in his reply:

> Will do. Luv u.

This morning, she dressed quickly and puttered around her townhouse, watering plants and dusting furniture as she waited to see whether he'd bother to show, given her bad attitude.

When he rang her bell, Indigo opened the door to his solemn face. He stared at her with puppy dog hazel eyes, but Indigo also noticed a hint of defiance. Usually, they greeted each other with a kiss, but this morning they nodded hello.

Max was wearing the navy slacks and the blue-and-white-striped collar shirt she had bought him on a recent shopping trip with a grad school girlfriend. She pursed her lips to keep from telling him how handsome he looked. She wanted to smooth his few untamed short curls and bless him with a reassuring smile, but she didn't.

Indigo knew Max hadn't meant any harm; he was trying to do what was right. Shelby had been insistent about that when Indigo called her in tears the evening she had fled from the photo studio.

"You know Max has a big heart," Shelby said. "Why would he block what comes naturally just because he happened to be talking to your brother?"

Indigo knew Shel was right, but she couldn't help how she felt. Max knew she was struggling to accept Reuben; he should have talked to her first. Instead, her future husband had had the nerve to make a decision that would deeply affect her without consulting her. Just because he could.

Max followed her down the sidewalk and held open the door to his SUV. He trotted around the vehicle and slid into the driver's seat. The radio in his ten-year-old Range Rover worked fine, but today he had it turned off. He remained silent and focused on the road.

It had been two days since the blowup, and Indigo was determined not to be the one to smooth things over.

She crossed her arms and settled back in the seat, fixing her stare ahead. It was a gorgeous autumn day, despite the oppressive humidity. She was thankful she had put her hair up in a bun, just the way Max liked it. She wondered if he noticed, but tried to convince herself she didn't care.

Max seemed to be trying to prove a point too—that he was

just as ticked off as she was. Every so often, she saw him glance at her, but she pretended to be unfazed.

They entered the church sanctuary and sat in a middle row of the middle section of pews just as three dozen robed adults filled the choir loft.

The service opened with prayer, and when Pastor Taylor strode to the pulpit with a Bible in hand and a grin on his face, Indigo knew they were in trouble. Sure enough, he asked the congregation to stand and he issued his usual command.

"Turn to the person next to you and hug him or her. Tell 'em, 'I love you today, tomorrow, and forever!'"

Great, Indigo thought. *Just great.*

Max winked at her and opened his arms. She stood there, debating whether to enter them, when Aunt Melba, who sat behind her, coughed.

Indigo reluctantly leaned toward Max and let him envelop her in a bear hug. She patted his back lightly and quickly stepped back, but not before he grasped her hands in his.

"I love you today, tomorrow, and forever, Indigo Irene Burns, soon to be Shepherd."

He looked into her eyes as he uttered the words and smiled. "Even if you're mad at me, nothing has changed."

Now she was angry at herself for being unable to stay mad at him. She sighed and hugged him again and leaned into his ear. "I love you too, Maxwell Edward Shepherd, even if I'm mad at you."

They took their seats and held hands.

A minute later, as the rest of the congregation was settling in, Aunt Melba tapped her on the shoulder and slid her a note.

> *I'm happy you two made up, but next time*
> *don't bring your fight to church, for everyone*

to see. You know how church folks can be. ☺
Enjoy the service. Love, M.

Indigo read the note again and passed it to Max. Aunt Melba was right—they were being too transparent, in front of friends and strangers. Apparently even Reuben had seen the exchange. He and Peyton sat on the pew behind her and Max, next to Aunt Melba. He had reached over during the fellowship period to shake Max's hand and had given Indigo a light hug. Reuben held her a few seconds too long for her taste, but then again, it was the first time she'd allowed him to embrace her since his move back home. She felt simultaneously uncomfortable and guilty, but also strangely at peace in her brother's grasp. Long ago, when they were kids, his hugs had been the only thing to soothe her when she was missing Mom Meredith and Dad David.

When she stepped back, his smile had been grateful.

Indigo assumed that Charles David was in the nursery, which accepted children five and younger. She had finally gotten his name right, and truth be told, the double moniker suited him. As cute and as energetic as he was, he didn't look like a Charles or a David, or a C.D.—he was a little old soul, a Charles David.

She turned her attention back to the service and squeezed Max's hand while a sweet soprano filled the air with a worship song. The lyrics touched her heart.

Here I am to worship.
Here I am to bow down,
Here I am to say that you're my God.

It wasn't the traditional gospel fare that the choir usually sang, but this solo rendition from Pastor Taylor's sister, who was visiting from Atlanta, was beautiful and piercing. And fitting.

They *were* here to worship God and to learn how to live better and love better. She looked at Max's profile as he watched the soloist bring the song to a crescendo and couldn't help herself. She leaned toward him and whispered in his ear.

"I do love you, Max. I'm still upset, but I do love you."

Max turned toward her and smiled. "I know you do," he whispered. "I love you back. And guess what? Reuben does too."

Indigo smirked and looked back to the next row. She peered squarely into Reuben's eyes. They confirmed what Max had just insisted. Reuben smiled at her, pointed to Max, and gave her a thumbs-up.

She returned her gaze to the pulpit without responding, but found herself amused that Reuben had apparently gotten caught up in her spat with Max, without knowing that her tantrum had been about him.

Max was right about Reuben; she saw it and felt it today, and she felt silly for being such a brat. But she wasn't ready to accept his affection or believe just yet that he was ready to truly fill the role of big brother. She wasn't going to get caught up in Reuben's fan club, even if they were in church. Reuben owed some answers to the entire family, especially to her.

10

Everyone just seemed to fit, including Reuben, Peyton, and Charles David. They were family, and all that mattered was being together. Reuben marveled at that realization when the Burns clan gathered at Mama and Daddy's house after Sunday service.

Daddy's blood pressure had stabilized in recent weeks, and he had been able to join Mama at church this morning. He looked satisfied and healthy as the men gathered in one area of the house and the women congregated in another.

Daddy settled into his favorite chair in the family room and was joined by Reuben, Max, Gabe, and Gabe and Rachelle's son, Tate, who had just completed an engineering internship in Michigan. Tate was home from college for a weekend break. The men watched ESPN and bantered back and forth about the skills of various golfers, basketball stars, and football players.

Peyton was in the kitchen with the ladies, immersed in helping finish preparations for dinner. Before he got too comfortable, Reuben decided to check on her. He strode down the hall and poked his head around the door frame, to get a full view of the kitchen. Peyton stood at the sink, washing lettuce and other vegetables for the salad.

Reuben chuckled and disappeared before anyone saw him.

Mama had given her a safe job. She didn't know that Miss Peyton could do the washing, the chopping, and the slicing, and could make a mean all-veggie or chicken salad in minutes. Everyone would learn over time how self-sufficient she was.

On his way back to the family room, Reuben glanced out the window and saw that Yasmin, along with Gabe and Rachelle's daughter, Taryn, had taken Charles David outside to play on his "Welcome to Jubilant" gift from Mama and Daddy. The redwood playset seemed monstrous for a preschooler. But Charles David beamed like he was in kiddie heaven as he moved from one section of the contraption to another. He went from swinging and crawling through the tunnel to scooting down the slide and climbing a miniature rock wall and back again.

Reuben shook his head. Mama and Daddy had gone overboard, if you asked him, but Peyton insisted that he needed to lighten up.

"When was the last time they had a little one around to dote on? This is their first grandchild since they gave up grandparenthood to raise you and your sisters," she told him. "Let them enjoy it."

Truthfully, Reuben was enjoying it as well. It meant a lot to see his wife and son so readily embraced by the family. Yasmin still had few words for him, but she hadn't been able to resist her nephew. Charles David had the temperamental teenager wrapped around his finger, and Yasmin had volunteered on her own to babysit. Reuben was beginning to think that she might be easier to connect with than Indigo. One way or another, he was going to form a bond with his sisters.

Back in the family room, the men were debating whether a top professional football player convicted of a felony would, or should, ever play again and whether another athlete known for losing his temper during games deserved his six-figure salary.

"He needs a pay cut for behavioral problems," Tate said.

"Naw, man," Gabe said. "He needs that extra money to get some counseling. He's a grown-up two-year-old, throwing tantrums just because he can get away with them."

Reuben took a seat and grabbed a handful of chips from the bowl on the coffee table. Before he could chime in on the conversation, Rachelle made the dinner call.

"Everything's ready! You guys can eat!"

Reuben led the way from the family room and bumped into Indigo, who was coming out of the bathroom. He paused and motioned for her to walk in front of him. "Ladies first."

Why was his heart thumping? This was his sister, and he'd been in her presence all morning at church.

"Thanks, Reuben," Indigo said and shifted her eyes. She lowered her head and quickly moved past him before he could think of a question or comment to launch a conversation.

He stuffed his hands in the pockets of his jeans and strolled toward the dining room, hoping he had mastered a poker face that didn't reveal his dejection. She hadn't yet acknowledged his willingness to participate in her wedding, which troubled him. He wanted to hear her say she was glad that he would be a groomsman.

Instead, it suddenly hit him why she and Max were making up in church today. They had been fighting, and maybe it was about him, and Max's invitation.

If Indigo didn't want him in the wedding, should he even bother?

11

Before Mama could orchestrate seating arrangements, Indigo strode to the end of the table closest to Daddy, to enjoy his company while he held court during the meal.

She patted the cushioned dining chair next to her, inviting Max to fill it. Max started in her direction, but Rachelle slid into the seat first.

"I'm not staying," she said to him and smiled. "Give me a minute and this spot is yours."

Rachelle leaned toward Indigo and lowered her voice. "I saw that exchange in the hall. Can you cut your brother some slack, Indie? Reuben is trying to reach out to you, and you keep pushing him away."

Taryn and Yasmin strolled into the dining room, behind a buoyant Charles David, who climbed into the booster seat his mother had placed in a dining room chair at the opposite end of the table from Indigo.

Indigo watched as Charles David hugged Peyton's neck and trusted her to secure him into his seat. She tried to resist the emotion invading her heart. If she fell for Charles David, then where did that leave her with Reuben? As cute as he was, she wasn't going to take the bait.

She wondered, however, whether the little boy knew that his

mother was blind and what a marvel she was to be so independent. The question led her to mentally check off the days until her next appointment with Dr. Woodman, her ophthalmologist.

It was time for her six-month checkup, to determine whether her early onset glaucoma was progressing. The condition had initially left her fearful that she'd find herself in the same position as Peyton, but in the four years since her diagnosis, she had been told that her glaucoma was under control. She had laser surgery every three years to keep her vision perfect enough to thrive without glasses.

Rachelle cleared her throat and Indigo realized her mind had wandered. She didn't want to have this conversation, though. When would people let up about Reuben?

She sighed and peered into Rachelle's eyes. "You don't know the whole story, okay? I'll fill you in later."

Rachelle tucked a piece of stray hair from her chin-length bob behind her ear. She looked skeptical. "If you always need an excuse to justify your actions, that's a sign that you may need to adjust them, Indigo."

She patted Indigo's knee and pushed the chair back far enough for Max to claim it. When she stood, Taryn motioned for her to join their family in the middle of the table. Taryn and Tate sat side by side, with Gabe to the right of his son. Rachelle pulled out a chair next to Taryn, and the picture was complete.

They looked so . . . perfect, Indigo thought. She knew the history of Gabe and Rachelle's once-turbulent marriage, though. The image before her hadn't come without some hard-won battles and a commitment to make their relationship a top priority.

Max settled in beside her and she sent an arrow prayer to God.

Will you bless Max and me with a beautiful family like that, Lord? Can the man I love and I always be solidly united?

It didn't escape Indigo that she was praying for marital unity when she and Max were currently out of sync. Forget about the future; they needed to figure out how to work together and have each other's back today. Max covered her hand with his.

"What was that about?" he asked, and motioned his head toward Rachelle.

"She misses having Taryn around all the time to advise, I guess," Indigo said and laughed. She didn't want to focus on Reuben right now. "The girl lives fifteen minutes away, in the campus dorms at Everson, but I guess to Rachelle that could be the other side of the world."

When the table was lined with dishes of food and everyone was seated, with Daddy at one end and Mama at the other, Indigo saw them exchange smiles.

"The whole family is here," Daddy said. "Can you imagine that?"

He turned toward Reuben who had somehow made his way to a seat across the table from Indigo.

"God is good, let me tell you!" Mama shook her head and waved a hand in the air.

Indigo held her breath. Mama was about to launch into a testimony, and unless someone stopped her, the food would be stone cold by the time she finished. Indigo and Reuben exchanged wary glances, and for the first time connected over something neutral. He grinned at her and she smiled, holding in the laughter that threatened to overtake her.

Daddy coughed and shook his head at Mama. "Tell us all about it after we start eating, Irene. Who wants to bless the food?"

Indigo smiled at him. "You do it, Daddy. It's been awhile since you've been able to be here with the whole family."

Daddy reached for her hand and nodded. "You're right, Indie.

Everybody bow your heads. Dear Lord, I don't know what tomorrow will bring, but I can tell you that I'm thankful for this day. I'm thankful to be healthy enough to join my family at the dinner table. I'm thankful to have all of my children here, safe and sound."

Yasmin, who sat at the other end of the table, near Mama, snorted. Indigo opened her eyes and scowled at the girl. Mama and Aunt Melba followed suit.

Daddy seemed oblivious to the interruption. "Lord, you promised in your Word to provide for our every need and to restore that which was lost. You said it and you have done it."

Indigo's stomach rumbled. Now she was ready for him to hurry it along.

"Lord, bless this food and this day, and bring everyone around this table closer together than ever before. Let this not just be a meal, but a time for bonding and sharing and creating lasting memories. In Jesus' name I pray, Amen."

"Amen!" Charles David said. "Let's eat. I'm hungry!"

Peyton laughed first and the rest of the family followed suit, even Indigo.

"Sorry," Peyton said when she had composed herself. "He doesn't let anything stand between him and a hot meal, and I think he has his eye on those rolls. He loves bread."

Indigo's eyes widened. She smiled at her sister-in-law in spite of herself, and in spite of the fact that Peyton couldn't see her expression. Clearly her other senses were extra keen.

"He got that honestly," Indigo said. "I'm trying to lay off the carbs so I can fit these hips into my wedding gown, but any other time, I'd be diving into them too."

Peyton smiled in Indigo's direction. When she did, her face radiated joy. Indigo had never considered locks a look she might want to try for her hair, but seeing how beautifully Peyton wore them gave her pause. There was something about this woman that was so serene and so self-assured, despite being blind and having to adjust to new surroundings, and despite having to spend time with her in-laws, including a sister-in-law intent on shunning her.

Indigo couldn't put her finger on it just yet, but whatever it was, it was appealing. As much as she wanted to have an attitude with Peyton, who was just two years older than her, she couldn't. If none of his other choices merited credit, Reuben had at least picked a great wife.

Indigo dug into the green beans, dumplings, and corn she had filled her plate with when the serving dishes circulated around the table. The aromas had been tempting her since she and Max had come over after church an hour or so ago. Max seemed just as focused on his plate, which he had piled high with a portion of every offering. Indigo chuckled when she realized that included sweet potatoes and mac and cheese.

"Is there a reason you're going overboard on the starches?" she asked.

Max grinned and took a bite of cabbage. "Just because I can. I only do this once a week, so I'm good."

"It's not as bad for you as you think," Mama said. "I'm cooking with lighter and healthier ingredients for your dad's sake. Yasmin doesn't like all that high-fat stuff either. She's a girl who keeps herself in shape."

"I didn't think you noticed, Mama," Yasmin said coolly. She took a sip of tea and glared at Mama.

Indigo was convinced she had either lapsed into a dream or Yasmin had lost her mind.

"I mean, why do you even care, since you don't think I'm ready to model? I would think you'd be trying to fatten me up. That would give you another excuse to keep me tied to your hip."

Daddy's eyes narrowed to a slit. "Watch it, young lady," he told Yasmin.

"Or what, Daddy? You two have already taken everything from me that matters."

Mama lowered her fork and frowned. "Now what are you talking about, Yasmin?"

Yasmin pulled an envelope from her back pocket and waved it at Mama.

Indigo looked at Max and pleaded with him through her eyes to do something. Max shook his head. She knew he'd say that. Whatever was about to happen needed to happen, in his estimation. Max didn't believe in glossing over reality or keeping secrets.

Doing just that had led to his parents' divorce when he was fifteen, and he made up his mind all those years ago that he would always speak the truth, in love. That way, no one would get blindsided or hurt by ulterior motives. He had lived that way ever since, he'd told Indigo, and had ended a few relationships with women who hadn't seen the harm in doing otherwise.

Indigo's own experiences with the devastating impact of hiding the truth had helped her appreciate Max all the more. Brian's revelation that he felt confused about his sexuality had shaken her to her core. Since their breakup, she tried to be real with everyone she considered a friend, and she expected them to be the same with her. Life was too precious and time too valuable to waste.

She was both eager and hesitant to learn where Yasmin was taking this conversation.

"Here." Yasmin passed a thick envelope to Mama.

Mama accepted it, and when she read the return address, her eyes grew wide. "Where did you find this, Yasmin?"

"Why did I *have* to find it, Mama? Why didn't you give it to me two years ago, when it came in the mail, addressed to me?"

Indigo felt like she was watching a tennis match—or the latest episode of *The Young and the Restless.*

Aunt Melba slapped the table with her palm. "Alright you two, that's enough. If this is a private conversation, take it into the other room. If you're going to talk about this in front of the family, get it over with and let's move on. Yasmin, stop being disrespectful and melodramatic. Whatever that letter from two years ago says, does it really matter now?"

Yasmin nodded. "It does, Auntie, because Mama's choice not to give it to me killed my dreams."

Yasmin sat back and folded her arms. She challenged Mama with her eyes to deny the charge. A single tear coursed down one of her cheeks.

Aunt Melba stared at Mama and waited. Mama looked at Daddy.

"Yasmin, sweetheart," Daddy said. "I don't know where you found it, but I believe that's a letter offering you a contract to spend two months modeling in Paris, for a famous designer's new line. We took one look at it and knew we couldn't let you go. We also knew that if we showed it to you, you'd insist on going. It was my decision to keep this information from you, not your mother's. We'd just slowed you down because your friends were getting into deep trouble while they modeled, and we just didn't feel comfortable sending you to Paris for two months without one of us being able to go."

"How could you, Daddy?" Yasmin said. "You snuffed the life out of my opportunity because it wasn't convenient for you and Mama to chaperone. How do you think that makes me feel? I can't be your baby forever. I just can't!"

Yasmin pushed her chair back from the table and fled the room.

"Ooooooh," a wide-eyed Charles David said in a loud whisper. "She's going to have to go to time-out."

Indigo was floored. Mama and Daddy had kept one of those big secrets that Max was always railing against. No one else knew what to say either, it seemed.

"Let's not let the food get cold," Mama finally crowed. "I'll talk to Yasmin later and clear the air between us. She'll be all right. We did what was best."

But Indigo wasn't sure. This was bigger than deciding to put the brakes on spot modeling jobs in Dallas and occasionally New York. Mama and Daddy had decided to disregard a once-in-a-lifetime opportunity without even exploring the options with Yasmin. For the first time in a long time, Indigo didn't believe her sister was being a spoiled brat or a drama queen.

She prayed that the girl wouldn't do something foolish just because she was angry. Some mistakes couldn't be repaired, but making more missteps worsened a problem.

Everyone slowly resumed eating, but the mood was glum. When Yasmin slammed the front door on her way out a few minutes later, Indigo's plans for dessert died. Charles David began to cry, and Mama did too.

12

Relief washed over Indigo three hours later when she responded to her ringing doorbell and found Yasmin leaning against the door frame.

"Girl, where have you been?"

Indigo wasn't surprised when Yasmin didn't answer. She grabbed one of her sister's wrists and tugged her inside. Yasmin clutched the letter, which now was a crumpled mess.

Indigo led her to the sofa, sat down next to her, and waited for her to share whatever she wanted. Instead, Yasmin sat back and folded her arms. She closed her eyes and leaned her head against the back of the sofa.

Indigo strolled to the kitchen a few yards away and paused in front of her open fridge. Yas may have missed dinner, but she wouldn't dare eat anything this late. Her bulimia hadn't been an issue in recent years, but everyone in the family knew Yasmin remained fanatical about her weight and about when and what she ate. As long as she was determined to model, this would come with the territory.

Indigo grabbed two cans of Diet Coke. She sat one on the glass table in front of Yasmin and popped hers open.

"You just gonna sit there and fall asleep, or are you gonna talk to me? I know you're hurt, but we can get through this."

Yasmin snorted, but didn't open her eyes or move. Indigo sighed, then took another swig of the beverage.

Truthfully, what could she say? She would be furious too if Mama and Daddy had pulled this on her. But what was done was done. She gazed at her sister—so pretty, yet so angry. So full of potential, yet distracted by what she couldn't change and couldn't have right now.

The longer Indigo stared at the thinner, younger version of herself, the more she remembered what it felt like to be a senior in high school, on the verge of independence, but choking under the hold Mama and Daddy had on her life. She realized in that instant that while her frustration had stemmed from conflicts over curfew and other efforts to break free from her parents' overprotectiveness, Yasmin's claustrophobia had to be more intense, because thanks to the brief period she had modeled, she had been given a glimpse of the world outside of Jubilant. She had experienced her longtime dream awakening, only to have it snatched away because her parents didn't understand or appreciate it.

Indigo couldn't apologize for agreeing with Mama and Daddy's decision to pull Yasmin out of the modeling world when it was clear that the kids she was working with had some troubling issues. But the offer of a modeling job in Europe, along with an invitation from one of the world's top designers to showcase his collection, shouldn't have been ignored or dismissed without exploring the options with Yasmin. One of them could have traveled with her as a full-time chaperone, even if for just that one show.

Indigo sat back on the sofa and laid her head back too. She stared at the ceiling and thought about the path Yasmin appeared to be traveling.

Mama and Daddy had shut her down to keep her safe from the evils in the modeling world, and Yasmin had defied their efforts anyway. The kids she was hanging out with now had questionable character and seemed to lack goals.

"Where have you been these past few hours?" Indigo asked, noting that it was almost 10 p.m. She should call Mama and let her know Yasmin was safe, but if she made that move, Yasmin would throw a fit.

"With my friends," Yasmin finally responded.

"And who would that be?" Indigo turned her eyes toward the girl. "These days, I don't know anymore. Cherita, Imani, and the other girls at St. Peter say you don't come around or call them anymore. And you never bring home your friends from school."

Yasmin released a sharp laugh that resembled a bark. "Trust me—Mama and Daddy wouldn't like them. Then I'd be left sitting in the house with my parents all the time, with nowhere to go and no one to go with."

Indigo sat up and faced her sister. "Yas, you know you're playing with fire, right? Hanging out with a tough crowd to get back at Mama and Daddy might hurt their feelings, but you're jacking up your life. Are you making yourself throw up after you eat? Smoking weed? Having sex?"

Yasmin frowned at Indigo. She looked embarrassed for a split second, before the expression changed to indignation. "Who are you now, Mama's clone or a Goody Two-shoes, bossy big sister? How dare you ask me stuff like that?"

Indigo shook her head. "How dare I not?" she asked. "You keep saying you want to model, yet look at what you've done to your hair."

Indigo pointed to the varying shades of dye that covered what had once been a lovely, healthy head of naturally black hair. While

Yasmin had maintained its length, the hair that framed her face was shorter on one side than on the other—cut into an asymmetrical, blunt style that Indigo wasn't sure whether Yasmin had gone to a salon to request or had cut herself.

"You keep blaming our parents for killing your career, but what are you doing to prepare yourself to launch it again when you do graduate from high school? You haven't mentioned applying to Everson or any other college. You haven't said anything about going to a modeling school or trying to establish yourself in some other way that can help you reach your goals.

"Instead, all I hear is the whining. All I see is you hanging out with people who can't encourage you to hold on to your dreams and be better, because it doesn't seem that they have any of their own. You lie down with dogs, Yas, and you are going to catch their fleas. That cliché ain't nothing but the truth."

Yasmin jumped off the sofa and headed for the door. Indigo leapt from her seat to block her sister's exit. She dashed around Yasmin and leaned her back against the door and folded her arms.

"You might run from Mama and Daddy, but you are not running away from me, Little Girl," she said between clinched teeth. She had never been this angry with her sister before, but watching Yasmin throw her life away was both infuriating and frightening.

"You can't keep dodging your problems. You have to face them, Yas, and you have to make some hard decisions. Who do you want to be? How will you make that happen? Get over the opportunities that have been wasted or missed. Concentrate on what you are able to do, and go after that with all of your heart. I am here. I will do whatever I can to help you. But I can't stand by and watch you self-destruct without saying something."

Yasmin balled up her fists and parted her lips to offer a reply, but as she formed the words, her eyes filled with tears. Instead of sharing what was on her mind, she covered her mouth with the palm of her hand to stifle her tears.

Indigo let her own tears flow freely and prayed that in this instant, God was touching her sister.

Please help me get through to her, Lord. Help her get back on the right track and let go of all of the pain and frustration she is feeling. I'm begging, Lord. Please.

Indigo approached Yasmin and stood before her, waiting for Yasmin to respond.

Yasmin lifted her head and looked into Indigo's eyes. Indigo flinched at the pain and fear she saw there. Yasmin, who stood about four inches taller than her older sister, leaned into Indigo for a hug.

"I do need your help, Indie. I want to do better so I can get back to doing what I love," Yasmin said, her voice swollen with tears. "I just don't know how. And I don't know how to forgive Mama and Daddy for being so controlling. Reuben can do whatever he wants without a word said, but they're hiding things from me to keep me from reaching my lifelong dream? I just don't get it. It hurts, and it makes me not trust them."

Indigo squeezed Yasmin's neck, then stepped back to take the girl's hands. How could she tell her sister she felt the same way about their parents' devotion to Reuben without stirring up more issues?

"They were wrong about the job in Europe, Yas. There's nothing else to say. But even so, you've got to find a way to prepare for your future and let that go. Hopefully they haven't kept anything else from you. You're in your senior year, so now is the time to begin focusing on what you can do over these next eight or nine months to be prepared after graduation. Concentrate on that, okay?

"When you graduate, you can start again. For now, just be

patient and do your best in school. And pray about Mama and Daddy. God can help you forgive them, and he can also help them support you more with your modeling, if that's what you decide you want to pursue after graduation."

Yasmin sighed and wiped her eyes with the back of her hands. "Thanks, sis. I guess that's all I can do for now."

She returned to the sofa and grabbed her Diet Coke before plopping down and reaching for the cordless phone. She extended the phone to Indigo, who hadn't moved. "Can you call Mama and Daddy and tell them I'm here? And if you'll let me stay overnight, can you tell them I'll be home sometime tomorrow? I just need to clear my head."

Indigo approached Yasmin and took the slim black phone. "Sure, Yas," she said and dialed their parents' number.

Indigo put the phone to her ear and waited for one of them to answer. She made a mental note to send Max a text. They spoke every night before falling asleep, to wish each other sweet dreams and sometimes pray together. She knew he'd understand her missing tonight. While she and Yas talked things out, he could be praying with and for them, on the other side of town.

13

Reuben shook himself awake and gasped for air.

He surveyed his surroundings and fell back on his pillow with a sigh. He was in his bed, in his new home, in Jubilant. He mopped the sweat from his brow and rubbed the moisture onto the sheet.

What had triggered the dream this time? When would the nightmares end, and was that even what this was? It had seemed so real.

In the dream, he'd been running from Mama and Daddy. The man and woman who chased him, yelling for him to come back or else, wore brown paper bags over their heads, with slits where the eyes, nose, and mouth were, but he knew it was his parents.

They were still hiding behind the image of being a perfect Christian family, despite Mama's drinking problem, Daddy's emotional distance, and Reuben's own angry outbursts behind closed doors. Everything on the outside was controlled, but when the masks came off, the truth would come out. Mama and Daddy were determined not to let him remove his.

As he ran away, images flitted through his mind of Mama stashing bottles of alcohol in her sewing room and Daddy grabbing his fishing pole and catching a ride with a friend down to the river, where he'd stay all day Saturday to remain out of the fray. Reuben saw himself, stuck in the house with two young girls, his sisters, begging him to jump rope, dress their dolls, or play patty-cake. He felt himself suffocating.

Then the scene switched, as it always did, to the dream/memory that had paralyzed him in recent years.

He was twelve years old again, riding in the backseat of his parents van, singing along to an old Stevie Wonder classic. His mother laughed when he messed up a lyric and turned in the front passenger seat to face him.

"No, baby, it goes like this . . ."

But before she could sing the verse, the van swerved and everything went black.

In his dream, Reuben watched himself wake up. He was disoriented and sitting inside the van, still buckled into his seat. He heard moans from his mother as she called out to him and to his father.

"David! Reuben, my baby!"

But Dad didn't answer. He sat motionless behind the steering wheel, with his head turned away from Reuben, resting in an airbag.

Reuben couldn't move, but he could see his mother, lying outside the vehicle a few feet away. She was bloody and groaning with pain.

He screamed for her: "Mom?! Help me!"

He fought to remove his seatbelt, but it was jammed, and the searing pain in his right arm rendered the arm useless. The passenger seat his mother had occupied had broken loose from its anchor during the impact, and while Reuben didn't feel any unusual sensations or achiness, his feet and ankles were pinned under it.

He called out to his mother again, and this time when she heard his voice, she seemed coherent.

"Somebody help us, please!" she yelled.

The sun was fading, but it wasn't dark yet. It looked to Reuben as if the van had careened down a hill. They were all alone, and the drivers of the cars speeding along the highway above didn't seem to notice the terrifying accident.

Mom continued yelling for help and praying aloud for what seemed like an eternity. His right arm throbbed and he wished he could cut it off. But more than his own discomfort, he was worried about hers.

Mom was always the one person in the family who wasn't afraid of spiders, roller coasters, or bloody knees. She held things together so she could take care of everyone else. Hearing her painful pleas worried him.

Eventually, her voice grew weak, and her tears subsided. She called out to him again. "Reuben, can you hear me?"

"Yes, Mom, I hear you. I'm scared. Are we going to be okay?" Reuben held his breath as he waited for her reassurance.

"Yes, baby, all of us are going to be okay. But Mom needs to close her eyes for a few minutes . . . Reuben? If Mom doesn't wake up . . . promise me . . . promise me you'll take care of Indigo and Yasmin, okay?"

Terror coursed through Reuben like poison. He almost vomited. He had to convince her to stay awake. "No, Mom! No! I need you and Dad! Don't leave me!!"

Mom shushed his cries. "It's okay, baby, don't be scared. You're gonna be fine. Someone's gonna find you soon. God has promised me. Now I need something from you: promise me that you will help Indigo and Yasmin remember us, and that you'll always be there for them, no matter what."

Reuben didn't answer. Sobs kept him from spewing an angry protest.

"Reuben? Mom needs to hear you make that promise, baby." Her voice was fading.

Reuben didn't want to. He wanted to yell at her and tell her she couldn't go. He wanted to hurt God for even thinking of taking her and Dad. But he knew Dad was already gone. He hadn't moved for a long time. Why did God have to take both of them? He was a kid. He needed them. He prayed that God would understand and change his mind.

"Reuben?"

He caught his breath and choked back the tears. "Okay, Mom, I promise. I will take care of my sisters. I'll always be there for them."

"And love them?"

"And love them, Mom."

Mom lay on her back in the brown patch of matted grass. Reuben saw her stare at the sky and sigh.

"I love you, Reuben. I'm going to sleep now, but you hang on. Someone is going to find you soon. I love you, baby."

Mom had closed her eyes then, and Reuben had screamed her name for hours, begging her to wake up. He pleaded with God to wake up both of his parents, or to let him go with them.

He yelled until well after nightfall, when two men carrying flashlights and a first aid kit found the van and worked feverishly to cut him loose from his seatbelt. He was hoarse by then, and his eyes were dry. He figured he must have cried all the tears his body possessed, but he hadn't stopped screaming until they put him in the ambulance and covered his mouth with an oxygen mask.

Reuben sat up in bed now and clutched the sides of his head. Sobs wracked his body again. Peyton stirred beside him and sat up too. She rubbed his shoulders and took his head into her lap. She stroked Reuben's cheek and let him cry.

When the tears abated, the deep sorrow he felt every time he had this dream was replaced by frustration. With himself.

"Moving back here isn't making it better," he finally said. "My sisters don't want to be bothered with me. I still can't keep my promise. I've never been able to do that. I let Mama and Daddy take over, and I never told them what I had promised my mom. I'm such a waste."

Peyton was silent for a long time. She pulled Reuben to a sitting position and wiped his tear-streaked face.

"I'm sorry you're still having bad dreams, baby, but they are getting better. I can tell. They aren't occurring as often as before, and you haven't had any panic attacks since our move. You will get to keep your promise, but it won't be in your timing, it's up to God," she said. "Just hold on and take it day by day. Your sisters aren't going anywhere. God will work it all out."

Peyton was tight with God. Reuben had never doubted that. When she declared how God would answer a prayer or resolve a situation, Reuben usually trusted her wisdom.

But something told him she might have misunderstood God this time. Being at the same dinner table, at the same family gatherings, and even in the same wedding, wasn't going to shrink the chasm between him and his sisters. And if Indigo and Yasmin ever learned about the promise to his mother that he hadn't kept, they would resent him all the more.

How could he fix that? How could he ever make things better? Reuben closed his eyes and sighed deeply. *Please, God, let Peyton be right. I hope you're on the case, working all of this out.*

Reuben hadn't trusted God much since the accident; but after this big move and the strain of these continued nightmares, he had nowhere else to turn. If the God Peyton loved couldn't fix things, he might never get well.

14

Indigo and Shelby strolled through The Galleria mall in Dallas, looking for just the right pair of heels to compliment the dress Shelby would be wearing tomorrow night when she joined her husband Hunt at a Sunday evening business dinner. The ladies had hit a few boutiques in the city and visited two other malls without success.

"Shopping is for the birds," Shelby told Indigo when they took a break between stores. They stood on an upper level of The Galleria, watching kids and teenagers ice skate below. "If I don't find what I'm looking for in one of the next few stores, I'll have to wear the standby black pumps I packed. At least they're peep toe. That's the style now, you know."

Indigo shook her head. This woman hadn't changed since their days at Tuskegee University. Indigo had been forced to dress both of them then, like she obviously was going to have to do today. Shelby was a naval officer through and through. She didn't have a clue, or even care, about the latest styles or the best designers or how and why she should stick with up-to-date clothes that flattered her gorgeous figure.

Four years after college graduation, her flawless cocoa skin, curvaceous shape, and beautiful smile could land her a spot on

America's Next Top Model, if the height requirement were adjusted downward and the age limit pushed up by a few numbers. Even without designer wear though, she dressed nicely and was comfortable and well put together in whatever she sported.

Still, Indigo chided her friend. "Shopping is wasted on you," she said. "You've tried on five or six fabulous pairs of shoes—stilettos, slingbacks, strappy sandals—and nothing suits you. You can't find what you want because you don't know what you're looking for! Will you just do what I say and buy a pair? Or two?"

Shelby laughed and patted Indigo's hand. "If it will help you chill out, then yes! Maybe we need to get down there on the ice and work off some stress?"

Indigo chuckled this time. "I am wound up pretty tight, aren't I? I should have warned you about that before you suggested that I come up to hang out with you while Hunt's in his meetings."

Indigo was thankful that this was one of her low-key weekends, free of photo gigs. She and Max had planned to house hunt, but he had been fine with changing their plans when she told him she had an opportunity to spend some time with Shelby. Though Corpus Christi was just six hours from Jubilant, it seemed a world away when they both were so busy. The much closer trip to Dallas was giving them some needed hang-out time.

Hunt had hit the ground running, networking and catching up with other engineers who had flown in from other sites. That left Shelby and Indigo on their own, to their delight.

They resumed their stroll through the mall, pausing occasionally to window-shop. When they reached an ice cream counter, Shelby tugged at Indigo's shirt and pulled her into the line.

"Let's take a break. One scoop of chocolate would do me good."

Indigo shook her head. "We aren't going to find you a pair of shoes, are we?"

Shelby laughed. "Spending time together, catching up, is much more important. Come on, forget about your diet today."

Minutes later, they were seated in the café court indulging their sweet tooths. Shelby's one scoop of chocolate had turned into two, and Indigo had followed suit.

Between savory bites, their chatter turned serious.

"So what have you decided about starting a family? Still think it's too soon?" Indigo asked. She had mailed Shelby and Hunt a congratulatory card for their third wedding anniversary two weeks ago.

Shelby scooped up some ice cream and slowly slid the spoon between her lips. She shrugged. "I do. He doesn't. He's ready to be a dad, and probably by the time a baby arrives, we would have been married four years. He thinks that's perfect."

"I thought you always wanted kids. What gives? Are you worried about your career?"

Shelby sighed. "I've always talked about becoming an astronaut, haven't I? I just don't know anymore."

Indigo suppressed the confused frown that would have mirrored the alarm in her heart. What was happening to her friend?

"Is everything okay between you and Hunt? Are you two alright?" She didn't mean to pry, but if Shelby needed to talk, she wanted her to know she could.

Shelby sat back and swished the spoon around in the half-eaten cup of ice cream, making it melt faster. "We're doing fine—finally. It's been an adjustment getting used to married life, especially as an interracial couple. Sometimes I feel threatened when I see his gorgeous blonde and blue-eyed co-workers flirting with him at office parties, and I wonder how far they push the envelope when I'm *not* around. Hunt is great, though. He always reassures me that he loves me, and he chose me to be his wife because that's who he wanted—me. But I do struggle with that, especially when I've had to go away on naval assignments for months at a time.

"What woman would leave her Brad Pitt–look-alike husband alone, when sharks are lurking?" Shelby said and laughed. "And then, to bring a child into the mix, with no family to help us in Corpus Christi, I just don't know. I'm debating whether to stay active duty or to pull back and join the reserves."

"What? Why would you do that?"

"That would allow me to be home more and also give me the flexibility I would need if we do start a family. I'm just scared about what these changes would mean for me and Hunt. I think he's convinced that having a baby will bring us closer together, but I'm not so sure. His family accepts me, for the most part, but I don't know how they would treat a biracial grandchild."

Indigo held up her hand before Shelby could say more. "You're dreaming up problems. Let's just take it one step at a time. Do you even want children?"

Shelby nodded. "Of course. I think so. Someday."

"Okaaay," Indigo said. "Do you want to continue flying planes? And what about your goal to become an astronaut? That's all you and Brian talked about when we were at Tuskegee. That's why you put yourself through that grueling training at Officer Candidate School the summer after graduation. You're going to give up on your dream, just like that?"

"I'm really not sure, Indie," Shelby said. "That just requires so much focus and time. Right now, I want to focus on my marriage more than anything else."

Indigo knew Shelby was holding back. Whatever it was, she hoped her friend would be okay. She took Shelby's hand in hers.

"If something's troubling you, give it to God, friend," Indigo said. “I’m always here if you need me. My only advice or feedback right now would be to listen to your heart, about everything. Don’t stop pursuing your goals just to accommodate someone else’s. Hunt knew you wanted to be an astronaut when he proposed. He knew you were black and you knew he was white.

“Ya’ll both knew your babies would be a beautiful combination of you both. Just hold on to those facts and try not to get lost in the fear so much. Okay?”

Shelby smiled and squeezed Indigo’s hand. “There’s the Indigo I know.”

Indigo smirked. “Now what is that supposed to mean?”

Shelby hesitated.

“You and I have always been real with each other, Shelby,” Indigo said. “Tell me what you mean.”

Shelby peered into Indigo’s eyes. “It’s just that you’re different . . . angrier . . . harder to get along with since Reuben has become part of your life again,” she finally said. “And I don’t mean since he moved back to Jubilant. This has been going on for a while. Now that he’s back in Jubilant permanently, you almost seem . . . bitter.”

Indigo felt her defenses rising, but tried to remain calm. “Well, I suppose I have had a chip on my shoulder.”

“But why? Do you even know?”

A laundry list of reasons filled Indigo’s mind—he was Mama and Daddy’s pet; they and everyone else thought he was so wonderful; he had never explained his long estrangement from the family; he seemed to feel like he was entitled to the praise and attention—after all, he was the eldest grandchild, and he was a miracle—he had been the sole survivor in the crash that had killed their parents.

Indigo felt knots forming in her stomach as she ran through

the mental list of aggravating circumstances. "Reuben's been walking around with a 'God complex' for a long time. I'm just tired of it."

Shelby opened her mouth to respond but seemed to think better of it. "Come on," she said. She stood and pushed her chair back from the table, and dumped her ice cream cup into a nearby trash bin.

Indigo did the same, and Shelby linked arms with her.

"Let's head back to the hotel and chat on the way. I'll wear the peep toe pumps. They'll be fine for tomorrow night."

On the drive to Shelby and Hunt's hotel suite twenty minutes away, Shelby kept her eyes on the road, but turned the conversation back to Indigo.

"Indie, I think it's you with the God complex."

"Excuse me?"

"You know I love you like a sister, so I'm only telling you what I see, from hours away in Corpus Christi. I'm sure Reuben has his hang-ups and faults—who doesn't? But he's not the one making Ms. Irene and Mr. Charles dote on him. He can't help that they treat him that way. He doesn't seem to come to town craving attention; he's just trying to get reacquainted with his family. I think his new job had more to do with that than anything else."

"So now you're on his side too. Just like Max, who refuses to un-invite Reuben to be in the wedding."

Shelby glanced at Indigo and reached over to touch Indigo's forehead with the palm of her hand.

Half angry and half hurt, Indigo forcefully removed it and tried to laugh. "Why are you checking my temperature? I'm not the sick one in this car," she said. There was an edge to her voice, despite the cheerful tone she managed to muster.

Shelby returned her hand to the steering wheel and weaved

in and out of traffic. The navigation system led her to the hotel, and she pulled into the parking lot. Indigo pointed to an empty spot next to her parked car. Shelby eased into it and pressed the button to automatically lower the windows before turning off the rental car.

Both women focused on the sea of vehicles whizzing by on the interstate in front of them.

"You know I love you, Indie, and I wouldn't intentionally say or do anything to hurt you," Shelby said. "But you've got to get past all of the attention Reuben is receiving and figure out how to forgive him over whatever he's done in the past to anger you. You also need to figure out what's making you feel that you have to compete with him so you can resolve that issue."

Indigo felt embarrassed. Shelby's lecture was similar to the wake-up call conversation she'd had with Yasmin two weeks ago.

"You and Reuben are different people and you weren't born with the same gifts or for the same purpose," Shelby continued. "Love him as he is, and allow him to do the same with you."

Indigo inhaled and slowly expelled the breath. She settled in the seat and folded her arms across her chest.

"What are you thinking?" Shelby asked. "Are you mad at me?"

Indigo shook her head. "No, I always want you to tell me the truth. This is your perspective. But I'm struggling with whether what you're suggesting is doable," she said. "I can't turn on and turn off my emotions like a faucet. I can't help it if I feel . . . I don't know what I feel! I just can't let Reuben in, just like that."

"Why not?" Shelby asked. "He's your brother."

The answer slipped from Indigo's lips before she gave it much thought. "Because if I let him get close, it will hurt even more when he decides to leave again."

There it was. The fear that had been lurking under the surface all along.

"Bingo," Shelby said softly.

Silence mushroomed between them for a long while, then Shelby spoke again. "Now that you've named the problem, you can move forward and resolve it."

That, though, might be the bigger problem, Indigo realized. What if she didn't want to resolve it? What if she decided to keep her distance, just in case her concern was justified? If Reuben were going to do another disappearing act, this time she would be prepared; this time it wouldn't tear her apart.

15

Reuben loosened his tie, then started the car. His first week on the job had earned him praise from his new boss and staff, and at the beginning of his first weekend as a Jubilant city employee, he was feeling great.

Working for a small agency was a massive leap from heading up a department for a worldwide entity like Amazon, but everyone was friendly and seemed to appreciate his knowledge. He was going to fit in nicely and have the chance to do a lot of meaningful work to get the city up to speed technology wise.

The fifteen-minute drive home gave him time to put to bed any lingering reflections over the day's meetings and loosely craft a plan of action for Monday.

His cell phone rang and jarred him back to the present. It was Peyton. He answered with his Bluetooth and simultaneously turned down his radio volume.

"Hey, babe," he said. "Are you and Charles David ready to go? I have to change into my jeans when I get home, and we can head over to Mama and Daddy's."

"We're ready," Peyton said. "I've wrapped Yasmin's gift from Charles David. He picked out a teddy bear when I took him to the mall earlier today. It would be great if you'd stop by a store and pick up a card for her, to hold the gift card we're giving her."

"No problem, I'll see you in a few."

"Great," Peyton said. "And Reuben?"

"Yeah, babe?" he asked, certain that she was about to venture where he didn't want to go.

"Have you decided yet what you're going to do?"

He had avoided the question all week, but he knew Peyton would ask before they left for this family gathering. She believed the frequency of his nightmares would decrease if he talked with his sisters about them, but he disagreed. Until he was ready to share everything, he would only look weak.

"Not yet, Peyton," he said. "I'll know when—or if—it's time to discuss what's been going on with them. Let's just celebrate Yasmin's birthday today. She's been having a rough time. I'm looking forward to seeing her smile."

He knew the admission that her "miracle survivor" brother wanted forgiveness for failing to keep a long-ago promise and the opportunity to honor that oath now wouldn't sit well with Miss Yasmin, especially after all these years. She had been a first grader when he left for college.

Revealing the truth to Indigo would cause a whole other ripple effect.

"I'll follow your lead," Peyton said. "Just know that there's never going to be a 'right' time for something like this. Once you let the truth out, God will provide the healing you need and everything all of you need to regroup and move forward together. I feel it in my bones."

Reuben smiled. "I married Pollyanna. You have more optimism than anyone I know."

Peyton chuckled. "I hear you trying to change the subject, Mr. Burns. I'll back off. See you in a few."

He ended the call and sighed.

Peyton was so great about letting him lead, even when they both knew she was right. But something wouldn't let him give in on this issue.

He wasn't ready to face more resentment from his sisters, no matter how badly he wanted those nightmares to end. He pulled into the parking lot of a drugstore and a few minutes later walked down an aisle featuring kids' toys and Halloween paraphernalia.

He paused, marveling at the variety of costumes they had crammed into such a small section. One in particular caught his eye—a mask with a square cheese head—Sponge Bob.

Reuben laughed and held it up to his face. Impulsively, he picked up a toy-sized mirror to check out how he looked.

The mask was too small, but the reflection in the mirror rattled him. He looked like a cast member in his nightmares, like one of the hiding parents in his dreams. Their masks were always paper bags with cutouts for the eyes and mouths. This square, cheese-colored mask was similar in shape and design.

Reuben's heart pounded.

Please, God, don't let me have a panic attack in this store. Please.

He stood there shaking, gulping air, and praying, and within a few minutes, his racing pulse slowed. He felt himself returning to normal.

Drained and angry, he dropped the mask back into the bin where he'd found it and went in search of the greeting card aisle. He continued to breathe deeply and acknowledged the message flitting across his mind: Until he found the courage to tell some hard truths, he really wasn't any different than the parents who haunted his dreams and tried to keep him trapped in their façade.

He couldn't control his thoughts while he slept, but he'd be darned if he was going to let his nightmares haunt his days too.

16

Reuben, Peyton, and Charles David showed up at Mama and Daddy's home ninety minutes later with their arms full of goodies.

Charles David insisted on lugging a gift-wrapped teddy bear nearly twice his size that he had picked out for Yasmin. He embraced the box and took one measured step at a time to keep from tumbling. Peyton held on to Reuben's forearm with one hand and clutched the greeting card that contained Yasmin's birthday gift with the other.

Reuben guided her and balanced a casserole dish of her vegetable lasagna. He had noticed a few frowns when Peyton announced what she'd be bringing to tonight's dinner, and with her usual perceptiveness, Peyton had picked up on their reaction.

"I know you guys like your food fried and refried," she'd said and laughed. "But give this a try. I bet you'll love it."

Reuben half hoped they didn't; that would leave more for him to take home.

He pressed the bell and greeted Mama with a kiss when she swung open the door. She stooped and opened her arms wide to envelop Charles David and the big gift.

"Don't crush it, Gramma!" Charles David said.

Mama raised an eyebrow and stood up. "Well excuse me, sir!"

She leaned over and kissed Peyton's cheek, then Reuben's before taking the lasagna from him.

"This smells good, Peyton," she said. "When do you find time to cook? Especially something like lasagna, when you're trying to keep up with Charles David?"

Reuben smirked. Mama wanted to add, "especially when you're blind?" but she was learning to restrain herself as she got to know Peyton and realized how little the disability impaired her daughter-in-law. Peyton's independence inspired Reuben but still caused him occasional anxiety. Not everyone was willing to be nice, just because someone was sight impaired.

Peyton was forever chiding him, though, along with anyone else who fretted on her behalf. "Second Corinthians 5:7, folks: I'm walking by faith and not by sight—literally," she would say. "This is my daily reality, and I'm in good hands."

She used her white cane when she needed it, and she had befriended the owner of a local taxi service, who had become a personal driver of sorts, picking her and Charles David up himself whenever she called the company to schedule transportation.

This evening, Reuben watched Peyton unzip her floppy leather purse and reach for her folded white cane when they entered Mama's foyer. Her fingers grazed it, but rather than grabbing it, Peyton pushed it deeper into the bag. Reuben grinned and read her thoughts: it wouldn't take her much longer to know how to navigate through this house without assistance. Today she would try maneuvering without the stick.

Peyton reached for Mama's elbow and let Mama lead her and Reuben into the kitchen. Charles David had already dropped his gift and run ahead of them.

Rachelle, Gabe, and Taryn greeted Reuben and Peyton with hugs and hellos. Taryn, who had left Everson College's campus to spend the evening with the family celebrating Yasmin's birthday, grabbed Charles David by the waist and peppered him with kisses.

"Yuck!" the pudgy-faced carbon copy of Reuben said and wiped his cheeks. He wiggled free from Taryn's embrace and ran toward the family room, where Mama kept his chest full of toys.

"Go on!" Taryn called after him. "We'll see how you feel about kisses a decade from now."

Daddy strolled in and waved hello to everyone. He approached Taryn and gave her a hug. "Thanks for gracing us old folks with your presence, Miss Taryn," he said. "You're here, but the guest of honor is not. Where's Yasmin?"

Mama turned away from the spaghetti she had just placed on a platter and rubbed her hands on her apron.

"She was in her room, on the phone and watching a movie on her iPod the last time I poked my head in there. I should probably go and get her, now that Reuben and the gang are here," she said. "Melba had a walk-in client at the hair salon, so she's going to be late, and Taryn's visit is a pleasant surprise. We hadn't planned for the college girl to give us some of her time!"

Taryn laughed and pushed her chair away from the table. She stood and headed toward the hallway. "I'm honored that you guys are honored by me!" she said and laughed again. "Let me go get Yasmin."

"Why is she holed up in her bedroom on her birthday, anyway?" Reuben asked. "She's eighteen; none of her girlfriends have offered to take her out?"

Mama and Daddy exchanged glances.

"That's a long story, one we'll save for another day," Mama said.

She began putting the food on the kitchen table and Peyton rose to help her.

"Sit down, Miss Peyton," Mama said. "I appreciate your manners, but this is easy. I'm just serving up the dishes everyone brought, including your lasagna."

"Where's the cake?" Rachelle asked. "And what kind did you make?"

Mama tilted her head toward the dining room. "Chocolate icing, chocolate cake," she said. "It was like pulling teeth to get out of her what she wanted, but she finally settled on her usual favorite."

"Good!" Peyton said and rubbed her hands together.

Mama placed a basket of French bread and two glass bowls filled with salad on the table. She motioned for Indigo to grab the salad dressing off the island, but Taryn appeared in the doorway, wide-eyed and breathless, before she could speak.

"What's wrong? Where's Yasmin?" Rachelle left her seat and walked over to her daughter.

"She's gone, Mom."

Fear coursed through Reuben and he saw Daddy's face fall.

"What are you talking about, Taryn?" Reuben asked.

"There's a note on her bed, on top of her pillow." Taryn's voice was trembling. "I read it, but I didn't touch it. Yasmin said goodbye. She wants to model again, and she says she's old enough now to legally do what she wants. I ran outside to see if I could catch her or see her leaving, but she's just gone."

"Oh." The simple, painful utterance escaped Mama's lips as more of a sigh than a word, before she collapsed in the chair Rachelle had occupied.

"Wasn't she in her room when we arrived?" Reuben asked. "She couldn't have gone far in twenty minutes."

Gabe shrugged. "I don't know, man," he said. "We've been here an hour. She said hello when we arrived and told us then that she'd come back out when dinner was ready."

Reuben pushed past Taryn, who was hugging her mother, and headed for Yasmin's room. The door was ajar, and sure enough there was a note on top of Yasmin's yellow butterfly pillowcase. Daddy came up alongside him and each of them read it silently.

> *Mama and Daddy, I'm 18 today so that makes me an adult, capable of making my own decisions and following my heart. Happy Birthday to Me! I've wanted to return to modeling forever, and I guess now's that time. I'm leaving to see if I still have what it takes to make it in the business. I believe I do. Please don't try to find me. I need to do this on my own, without being sheltered or treated like a baby. I'll be fine, and when I'm ready I'll be in touch. Love You Always, Yas*

Daddy sat on the bed, bowed his head, and covered his face with one of his hands. "This is going to kill your mother. Just when we get you back, we lose another child. My God."

Reuben felt broken too, but for a more selfish reason. How could he keep his promise if Yasmin were gone? He had come home to get to know her, to take care of her, and she had decided to leave?

He sat next to Daddy on the bed and put his arm around him. He was at a loss for words. Fear for Yasmin's safety competed with anger at her arrogant foolishness and despair over his inability to fix this.

He looked up and found himself unexpectedly peering into

Indigo's eyes. She stood in the doorway clutching a gift bag and biting her lip.

"Tell me that girl didn't run away," she said.

Reuben rose from the bed but didn't move toward her. He wasn't sure what to say, so he beat himself up more. If he had kept the promise he made to his mother nearly twenty years ago, he, Yasmin, and Indigo might be in very different places. They still would have been closely connected to their grandparents, but maybe, just maybe, their sibling bond would have filled any void.

Now, Yasmin was out there on her own, trying to be Miss Independent, instead of trusting in and relying on the people who loved her most, including him.

Reuben couldn't recall whether Indigo had ever seen him cry, even when they were kids, but suddenly it didn't matter. He couldn't play the strong big brother right now. Tears coursed down his cheeks, dripped from his chin and disappeared. He let them.

"I'm sorry," he told Indigo.

She approached him and sighed. "I am too, Reuben, I am too."

Indigo opened her arms and hugged him, and his silent weeping threatened to become sobs. She did still love him, after all.

17

The rest of the evening was a blur of cell phone calls and frantic conversations from just about every room in the house. The family contacted anyone they could think of who might be able to help find Yasmin. Indigo went from room to room, trying to contain her nervous energy.

She stood nearby as Gabe called a golfing buddy who was a cell phone executive, and asked if Mama and Daddy could trace Yasmin's whereabouts through her mobile phone.

"Only if she uses the phone to make some calls," Gabe said. A quick online check of the bill indicated that she hadn't done so yet.

Rachelle and Taryn called teenagers from the church youth group who attended school with Yasmin, hoping they might know the names and neighborhoods of her current friends.

Indigo flushed with shame as she listened to them pepper the girls and guys with questions. If she'd been a better sister in recent months, she would know the answers to some of these questions herself.

An hour into their efforts, Indigo saw Rachelle's optimism fading. Her youth group members couldn't give her anything more than nicknames and promises to look through their yearbooks for pictures of Yasmin's friends that would provide their legal names.

"Who knows if this is even worth researching, though?" Taryn asked Indigo. "We don't know for sure that she left with someone else. She might have taken off on her own, or someone who isn't even from this area could have helped her. Who knows who that girl has been hitting up online."

Indigo nodded. "Whatever the case, I know she's headed for Dallas, where she's modeled before, or maybe even New York, which would be absolutely crazy with no place to stay."

Indigo's eyes widened with a revelation. "Where's Mama? Maybe she can track down some information on Yasmin's old modeling buddies. I bet she'll try to look one of them up and see if she can crash at their place in New York."

When she couldn't find Mama in any of the other rooms in the house, Indigo trotted down the hall to her parents' bedroom, but paused outside their closed door. After a few seconds, she knocked and waited, but neither of them answered. She stepped back and flipped the hallway light switch off.

The bedroom light was on. Why weren't they responding? Indigo knocked again and this time called them.

"Mama? Daddy? You in there?"

Daddy opened the door a few seconds later, and stepped aside so Indigo could enter. Mama was on her knees, with her elbows perched on the edge of her bed and her hands clasped for prayer. Her eyes were red and she looked stricken.

Indigo wanted to tell her it would be okay; no one had died. But she knew that's exactly what Mama feared, so she didn't go there.

"You find out anything yet?" Daddy asked.

Indigo shook her head. "No. I wanted to talk with you two to see if you still have contact information for her model friends in

New York. I'm guessing she may have tried to reconnect with one of them, if she's planning on resuming her career."

Mama nodded. "I had the same thought, Indie. She took her address book with her, which must have that information, along with the wad of cash she's been saving from babysitting jobs for a good five years. I called the bank and checked her account balance. It's down to $10."

Mama sighed. "All that money. I guess she may have gone to New York. She has more than enough to cover a plane ticket and expenses for a month."

Indigo raised an eyebrow. "Just how much does she have? Remember the cost of living in New York, from my grad school days, Mama. A month's worth of living expenses in Jubilant equals about two weeks' worth in the Big Apple."

"She had about $3,500, according to the last bank statement I reviewed with her."

Indigo plopped on the chaise lounge near the window and shook her head. "And she had easy access to all that money? Why?"

As soon as she uttered the question, Indigo wished she could retrieve it. Mama and Daddy's faces fell. She saw guilt pool in both their eyes. She slid off the seat, walked over to Daddy, and hugged his neck.

God, please don't let all of this drama make his blood pressure skyrocket. Keep him on track.

"You and Mama are the best," she said softly in his ear. "Yasmin has made a choice out of youthful pride. She'll wake up and come around. I'm going to keep trying to reach her, okay?"

Daddy stepped back and kissed her cheek. He took both of Indigo's hands in his. "We spoiled both of you rotten, but we couldn't help it," he said thickly, fighting off tears. "You were our princesses—the daughters we never had. Your father was a great son, but he was our only child. When he died . . . something in me died. You two girls and your brother gave me some hope . . . a reason to want to keep living."

Daddy's voice trailed off, but Indigo was stunned. These were the most sentences she'd heard him string together, outside of prayers. Ever. He was scared.

She stared at him, unable to speak, but hoped he saw the love in her eyes. None of them could control this. Yasmin had put herself in a foolish and dangerous situation, even if she were eighteen. Being a green, eager model wannabe in any cosmopolitan city in this country could lure the attention of all kinds of scam artists . . . and criminals.

Prayer—and each other—was all they had right now.

Daddy obviously agreed. "Even good things come out of storms." He squeezed Indigo's hands, which were still resting in his. "I saw what happened between you and Reuben today. After all these years, you're finally brother and sister again. Now we've just got to get the baby of the family home."

Indigo gave him a reassuring smile, but she wished her heart were smiling too. She had put aside her anger and resentment because this unfolding drama was more important. Still, nothing had been resolved. She wanted and needed answers from Reuben to be at peace with his return and his newfound commitment to the family. She hadn't been able to shake that desire.

For the time being, though, she needed Reuben as much as he apparently needed her, and if this temporary truce gave Daddy some peace of mind, all the better.

18

Reuben ended the call and turned to face his family.

"Mayor Henning says legally there's nothing we can do. Like Chief Richardson told Aunt Melba, the police's hands are tied too, unless we suspect foul play. Looks like Yasmin is grown and gone, for the time being."

His news settled heavily in the gloomy silence. It was just about midnight, and everyone had gathered in the family room to update each other on what was turning out to be their lack of progress and to discuss what the next step should be.

"I don't know that there's anything we can do, but pray that she'll come to her senses and at least have the decency to call us and tell us she's okay," Aunt Melba said. "That child, that child."

Aunt Melba ran a hand over her short, layered 'do and closed her eyes. She leaned back on the sofa, next to Peyton, and began humming "I Surrender All."

Mama, whose eyes were still red and who hadn't spoken to anyone since learning the news, sat next to Melba and bowed her head. Peyton, Max, and Gabe joined in the humming. Rachelle and Indigo did too, until this unlikely chorus filled with harmony, and some off-key participants, created a haunting melody. It seemed as if they were moaning to God.

Seeing his family in pain, yet in one accord asking the Lord to handle this situation, caused an emotion Reuben couldn't identify to swell inside of him. He didn't talk to God every day like Peyton did. Yet this particular hymn unnerved him. It was the same one Mom Meredith regularly sang in church before she died. He felt his heart beating faster and beads of sweat forming on his brow. What was happening today? Why were the demons that he usually kept at bay until he slept trying to invade his waking existence?

Reuben jammed his hands into the pockets of his jeans and strode out of the room, down the hall, and out the front door. Night had fallen, but he preferred to be cloaked in its darkness right now. He stood on the porch for a few minutes, breathing in and out, then plopped down on the swing and continued trying to regulate his breathing. He couldn't have a panic attack right now. He couldn't handle the embarrassment, and his family didn't need any more drama. He kept breathing slowly, in and out, and tried to stabilize his heartbeat. He felt twelve years old again—helpless, scared, and unable to control his fate, or that of the people he loved.

Tonight, though, he realized he was afraid because Yasmin's birthday gift to herself—her flight to so-called freedom—would forever change the Burnses. Even if she came home tomorrow, nothing would be the same.

Reuben wasn't sure why he felt so strongly about this, he just knew. He wasn't sure if the change would be good or bad, helpful or harmful; but it was sitting on the horizon and he knew he had to be ready. They all did.

When his heartbeat was normal again, he was able to focus on his surroundings. Reuben nudged the swing into motion and enjoyed its slow, back-and-forth rhythm. He listened to the mosquitoes buzzing near him and stared at the inky sky. Minutes later, he turned his eyes toward the door when it creaked open. Max stepped onto the porch and leaned against the doorway.

"You alright, man?"

"Not really," Reuben said. He hadn't known Max long, but he sensed that he wouldn't go wrong in trusting him. "I come home and this family starts unraveling."

Max shrugged and walked over to the edge of the porch, where he too looked up at the stars. "That's a stretch. What does your coming home have to do with Yasmin's leaving? She didn't mention you in the letter. This was all about her modeling career."

Reuben followed Max's gaze. "I'm not so sure. I think she left because she was suffocating. And when I was eighteen and living here, I was too. She ran away and left a note; I went to college and never came back. I was able to hide my disconnection better, but it was running away, all the same."

Reuben looked at Max and tried to mask his despair. "If she's anything like me, I don't think she's coming back, Max. She's searching for something bigger than a modeling career, and just like I once did, she thinks she has to leave to find it.

"Truth is, we need to find out what's wrong in here," Reuben pointed to his heart, "and figure out how to fix that, so we can stop this pattern in our family. I don't want Charles David doing this to me in another fourteen years."

Max frowned. "Why do you call it a pattern?"

"Because it *is* a pattern in this family." Rachelle appeared in the doorway and answered before Reuben could respond.

"I didn't mean to eavesdrop. I was coming to check on you, Reuben," Rachelle said. "I couldn't help but overhear the two of you talking."

She stepped onto the porch and faced the two men. She looked from Reuben to Max and hesitated.

Max turned to head back inside. "Looks like you two need to talk privately. I'll go check on Indigo."

But Reuben stopped him. "Stay, man. I trust you. Just don't let whatever you hear change how you feel about my sister."

A wry grin spread across Max's face. "She's familiar with my skeletons too. It's all good."

Rachelle sat next to Reuben on the swing and faced him. "We like to keep the Burnses' skeletons hidden until the bones decay," she said. "The trouble with that is that the rotting smell gives away the hiding places anyway.

"I don't have any deep, dark secret to share, but as I heard the last part of your comment to Max, about the Burns children running away and it being a pattern, I got chills.

"I felt like my parents were too controlling, so I left Philadelphia and came all the way to Jubilant, Texas, for college. Your father David was my first cousin. When he was sixteen, he ran away one weekend because Aunt Irene and Uncle Charles wouldn't let him join a school band that practiced on Wednesday nights, when he was scheduled to be at Bible study. David came back after spending a couple of nights at a friend's house. He never ran away physically again, but he never allowed himself to develop a relationship with God, because he thought all the rules of being religious would keep him from performing the music he loved. That's why he moved his family to New Orleans, to be close to the jazz scene and far from the pressure to be so holy and perfect."

Reuben settled back in the swing. He felt as if the air had been sucked from his body.

Rachelle sat back too and turned her gaze toward the sky. "I almost didn't share that with you, thinking tonight was rough enough, but you know what? We've got to stop trying to protect each other in this family and just get real. The more real we are, the more we can hear what each other's needs are and do our best to meet them. I just thought you needed to know that, because it's part of your history, and part of who your father was, and who we all are."

Reuben leaned toward her and hugged her. "Thanks, Rachelle."

He wasn't sure whether he was thanking her for telling the truth or for simply caring enough to share something about the father he didn't remember as much as he wanted to. One thing was certain: he wasn't the only member of this family struggling to get whole, and it was clear that none of them could do it alone.

19

Any other time, she would have said yes before they finished making the offer. This afternoon, Indigo's hand shook.

She didn't know if she could go to London for a photography shoot with her sister missing. She just didn't know.

"Um . . . let me check my calendar and get back to you, okay?" she told the magazine editor.

He didn't respond, and she knew he was offended. Nobody took time to "think about" a job when this prestigious publication called. Indigo was certain the editor was thinking that if she didn't know this, she wasn't the right person for the job.

"I'd love to do it, of course, but my family has some personal matters that we must attend to in the coming weeks, and I just want to make sure this doesn't overlap."

Indigo put him on hold and laid her forehead on the table. What should she do?

Yasmin had been gone for four days and hadn't called or sent any text messages. Worst-case scenarios sped through her mind, again.

Please, God, tell me what to do.

The silence that enveloped her left her cold. She needed to make a decision now.

Max strolled into the studio from the dark room and waved instead of speaking when he saw she held the phone in her hand. He frowned when he realized she wasn't talking.

She lifted her head. "I've got Erich Sierdhoff on hold. He wants me to shoot a new gallery display at a museum in London for *Ultier* magazine. It's a four-day job, though, and I'm not sure if I should be leaving the country with Yasmin still missing."

Max perched on a stool across the room from Indigo. "When would you have to leave?"

"Next week, on Wednesday or Thursday."

"How will your being here help?"

Indigo hesitated. "She might reach out to me. She might need me. She may be in trouble, and I don't want to be half a world away."

"But what if she doesn't reach out to you? What if she isn't in trouble? What if she really is trying to make it on her own?"

Max's nonchalance about her sister's flight was making her angry, but she had a client on hold. She pressed the red button on the phone.

"Hello, Erich? If we can shorten the job from four days to two, it looks like it's doable for me. Is that suitable?"

"Sure, Indigo," Erich said. "We've admired your work since seeing your winning shots from last year's New York Photo Awards. We're looking for a fresh eye to shoot these iconic fine art offerings, and felt like you would fit the bill. Give me your address and we'll get the contract to you ASAP. We'll fly you out a week from now, out of Houston."

"That's great," Indigo said.

She ended the call and exhaled. Instead of rejoicing that her work was landing her greater recognition and new clients, she felt sick to her stomach. How could she celebrate anything when her baby sister was missing?

Max approached her and took her face in his hands. He leaned toward her and kissed her lips, then her forehead. "You have to keep moving, for Yas. If she ever thought her efforts to pursue her dreams had killed yours, that would destroy her."

Indigo wrapped her arms around his waist and hugged him. She laid her head on his chest and closed her eyes. How did he do that? Somehow he read her like a book and answered the questions swirling through her mind before she could articulate them.

She knew Max was right.

"You have to live the life God gives you and pray for others to find him in their own way," he said. "But your feeling obligated to sit out of the game isn't serving anyone. It could be that the jobs you land lead you right to her. Just keep praying and doing what you're supposed to do."

On one hand, his advice seemed coldhearted and selfish; on the other, it revealed the maturity and grace her life should be reflecting as she sought to trust God more. That was another thing, though. Did she really trust him like that, or was she just giving lip service to the notion because Max fully believed?

Indigo didn't have time to sort it all out now. She was going to London and that was that.

The phone rang before she could psychoanalyze herself further. She pulled herself away from Max and picked it up to read the phone number.

"Hey, Mama, everything okay?"

Indigo's heart pounded. Max held on to her.

"Nothing's wrong, Indigo," Mama said. "I just picked up the mail and received a letter from the Jubilant Women's Foundation.

They want to honor me as Woman of the Year for my work in educating youths about the pitfalls of addiction. Can you believe that? Me?"

Indigo's heart swelled. This award was a big deal, in Jubilant and beyond. She covered the phone and looked at Max.

"Mama's won a big award," she whispered, before resuming her conversation. "Good for you, Mama. Why do you sound so ambivalent about it?"

"My youngest child has run away and they're trying to honor me as Woman of the Year? I think they've got it wrong. If Yasmin doesn't come home soon, I'm going to have to give my regrets."

Indigo turned toward Max again. She thought about the advice he'd just given her. She wished she could hit a playback button for Mama.

If Mama declined the honor because of Yasmin's choices, that meant a city full of youths who needed to hear her story of overcoming alcoholism and a drunk driving charge might miss the chance to be encouraged that even when you make serious mistakes, you can start over.

But how did one stay engaged in life and not get weighed down by it? Max seemed to have figured it out. Now, if he could just bottle that wisdom and give it away. She'd be first in line to buy.

20

Indigo pulled into the parking lot of the squat brick building and climbed out of her eight-year-old black sedan. She checked her watch to see how late she was and trotted to the door of Hair Pizzazz.

Aunt Melba was going to kill her. Usually if she were more than ten minutes late, she risked having to reschedule. But she was leaving for the job in London in two days; maybe her favorite aunt would cut her some slack. Aunt Melba was considering retiring and selling her business. These days, she only scheduled clients on Tuesdays and Wednesdays, so every slot was golden.

Indigo would multitask during today's visit to the salon, because Melba had promised to help her with wedding logistics, and Rachelle was taking a long lunch from her optometry practice to join them.

Mama was still understandably upset about Yasmin's disappearing act, and the only thing that seemed to be taking her mind off of it was spending time with Charles David. When the youngster wasn't at her house, she was visiting Reuben's home to get her fix. In the meantime, everything else was waylaid, including preparations for Indigo's special day.

Last Sunday, Mama hadn't bothered to go to church or prepare dinner for their usual after-church family gathering. She had stayed home in bed, complaining of a headache. Rachelle and Gabe had hosted it instead, and Indigo had fretted the entire time whether Mama was lapsing into her old behavior of drinking and hiding.

Regardless of whether her imagination was running wild or there was some validity to her concerns, asking Mama about invitations, favors for wedding guests, and flower choices would be a waste of time when she was so preoccupied. But as they had promised, Rachelle and Aunt Melba were ready and willing to assist her.

Indigo swung open the door to the salon and grinned at the life-sized portrait of a glammed-up Aunt Melba that graced the foyer. Indigo had taken the picture four years ago, after Aunt Melba recovered from her stroke and resumed control of the salon. The photo was Aunt Melba's pronouncement that she was back and better than ever.

Indigo was usually humble about her work, but every time she saw the photo, she gave herself kudos for capturing her aunt's vibrant essence in still life. The picture was also Indigo's reminder of how far she had come. There were days that summer four years ago, when she sat behind Hair Pizzazz's reception desk scheduling appointments and running the business side of the salon while Aunt Melba recovered, fretting over whether her life would ever move forward. Her summer newspaper internship had come to an abrupt end when she was diagnosed with glaucoma, she feared that the eye issues would kill her photography career, and she worried that she liked her then-fiancé Brian more than she loved him.

Funny how God worked everything out.

Indigo had formally met Max right here in this salon, when God provided part of her deliverance—a winning entry in an *O*

Magazine photography contest featuring pictures of customers she had snapped while running the salon.

Those memories enveloped her whenever she stopped by Hair Pizzazz. The enlarged photo of Aunt Melba was her regular reminder to be thankful, and to trust that God was working out all of the details. Funny that she thought about that now, when everything in her life that mattered seemed unwieldy again. She knew by now to let go and trust God; why didn't she just do it?

Raven, an Everson College student who served as one of Aunt Melba's part-time receptionists, greeted Indigo when she finally pulled herself away from the portrait and approached the check-in desk. Raven picked up the phone and informed Melba that Indigo had arrived.

She chuckled as she ended the call. "Melba says your time has expired, but it's your lucky day. Her one o'clock client called to reschedule, so come on back and eat crow."

Indigo rolled her eyes and laughed. "That woman is something else."

She strolled to the shampoo area and opened her arms wide as she approached Aunt Melba. "Give me some love, Auntie! Thank you for fitting me in."

Aunt Melba put a hand on her hip and smirked. "Ummm hmmmm. Sit your little self in this chair so I can get this hair washed and styled before you get me behind schedule for real."

Indigo laughed. "Thanks, Aunt Melba. Is Rachelle here?"

"She's in the back, having lunch. Let me wash your hair and while you're under the dryer, the three of us can chat."

Aunt Melba nestled Indigo's neck in the U-shaped crook of the shampoo sink and tilted her head back. When the warm water coursed through her hair and down her scalp, Indigo breathed deeply and relaxed her tense shoulders. Usually she chattered, but today, she cleared her mind and let her thoughts settle.

Aunt Melba helped her sit up and towel dried her hair. Indigo wasn't surprised that she had noticed the silence.

"You okay?"

"I don't know," Indigo said. She didn't have to put up a front when she was here. Aunt Melba and Hair Pizzazz were a refuge.

Aunt Melba slathered conditioner on her hair and laid her back, to rest her head in the sink while it worked.

"Let me blow dry and style Mrs. Easten, and then I'll have an hour window with just you and me. Rachelle can join us and we can get caught up on everything."

Indigo nodded and closed her eyes.

The next thing she knew, Aunt Melba was standing over her again, rinsing her hair with warm water and massaging her scalp.

"I must have dozed off," Indigo said and stifled a yawn. She saw Rachelle sitting across from her, flipping through a stationery catalog.

"You actually took a fifteen-minute nap," Aunt Melba said and smiled. "Guess you needed it."

Indigo smiled. "I guess so. I've had a lot on my mind—as we all have—and I haven't been sleeping well. But maybe the trip to London will get me back on track."

"Don't put yourself under that kind of pressure," Aunt Melba said. "Stop trying to fix everything and just take it one day at a time. We're going to get through this."

Rachelle walked over and sat in the seat with the shampoo bowl next to Indigo. "You're trying to plan a wedding, keep your career going, deal with the disappearance of your sister and the return of your brother. You aren't superwoman, Indigo."

Melba towel-dried Indigo's hair and helped her sit up so she could comb through it.

"Why'd you throw Reuben in the mix? What's he got to do with anything?" Indigo asked Rachelle.

Rachelle and Aunt Melba exchanged glances.

"Child, you can't see the forest for the trees, can you?" Aunt Melba asked. "We saw the mini-reconciliation between you two after Yasmin took off, but we've seen the animosity you've had toward Reuben much longer. Whatever you've been feeling couldn't have gone away overnight."

Indigo sighed. They knew her too well.

She looked from one to the other and tried to quickly formulate a defense. Instead, she crumbled in tears. Aunt Melba combed through her hair while she cried. When Indigo was spent, Melba gave her a clean towel to wipe her face and Rachelle handed her a small paper cup of water.

"Let's skip the dryer today. I'll blow it dry so we'll have more time to talk," Aunt Melba said.

Indigo composed herself and followed Melba over to her stylist station, where she sat in the elevated swivel chair. She expected her aunt to stand behind her and get to work. Instead, Melba pulled two chairs in front of Indigo and motioned for Rachelle to fill one of them.

"Feel better now that you got those bottled up tears out of your system?" Aunt Melba asked.

Indigo shrugged. "I guess. I don't know."

Rachelle sighed. "You've got a lot on your shoulders right now, young lady. A lot. But I do believe God is going to give you the strength to handle it all. Some things are out of your control. We're all praying for Yasmin and putting out feelers to find her. That's the best we can do without having any idea of which direction she might have headed. New York City is so big, we need to pinpoint something."

Indigo kept her indignation under wraps. If this were Taryn or Tate, she was certain Rachelle would be pulling out all stops. But she couldn't fault her cousin's perspective on this; Yasmin had made this choice. Even if they did find her, they couldn't legally make her come home, since she was now eighteen.

"Then there's Reuben. I'm still not understanding why you've been so angry at him," Rachelle said and frowned. "He decided to move his family here to be closer to all of us, and no matter how much he tries to reach out to you, you continue to ostracize him. What gives?"

Indigo took a sip of water and tried to quell the anger and frustration she felt welling up. "You don't understand, Rachelle. This is so much deeper than what you're seeing now—today. When Reuben left a long time ago . . ." Her voice trailed off. She wasn't sure she could revisit those memories and articulate her pain without spiraling into tears again.

She took a deep breath and shook her head. "There's some history there that I just don't want to deal with right now. But yes, I'm angry at him, and I'm doing my best to forgive him and move on, because I know that's what he and I both need to happen. That's what Mama and Daddy need, and Yasmin too. If I were on better terms with Reuben, Yasmin would have been too. She only had an attitude with him because I did."

Rachelle held up a finger. "Let me run to the car—I'll be right back."

When she returned, she carried a gift-wrapped package which she placed on Indigo's lap.

Indigo frowned. "You're giving me a gift because I'm at odds with my brother?"

"Just open it," Rachelle said. "It's a journal that I was sending to the daughter of a friend who starts a creative writing graduate program in a few weeks. I thought she'd appreciate the gift as a place to store her personal thoughts, unrelated to her coursework. But I want you to have it. You need it."

"Why?"

"Because whenever you're holding something inside that you're afraid to explore or too emotional about to speak the truth to, you need to find another way to release it, Indie. Pick up a pen and this journal every day and just spend five minutes thinking about your relationship with your brother and dumping your thoughts, anger, and fears there. You know what? You can even talk to God on paper. He'll receive it."

Indigo hadn't kept a journal or a diary in years, but Rachelle was right—she needed a way to release her pent-up frustrations so she wouldn't find herself experiencing another unexpected crying jag. She needed to figure out what she wanted to say to Reuben, even if she never shared her feelings with him directly.

She tried to smile. "Thanks, cousin. Maybe I can do some of this en route to London."

Rachelle looked skeptical. "Maybe, but you may prefer to do it in privacy. Trust me—you don't know where your writing will take you. The stuff that comes out may surprise you or horrify you. You need to be in a place where you can privately deal with whatever comes up. It will be good for you though. Very cathartic. I've been there."

Indigo nodded. "Gotcha."

Aunt Melba pulled out the wedding stationery brochure and turned to a list of reception favors in the bridal magazine. "Now, on to the things we can help you do today," she said. "Let's quickly look through here and pick out our top three favorite invitations and reception trinkets, then I'll blow dry and style your hair while we discuss them, okay?"

Indigo felt lighter than she had in days, maybe weeks. She stepped out of her seat and hugged Aunt Melba and then Rachelle. "You ladies are my angels. All the time."

They pooh-poohed her mushiness, but Indigo could tell that her praise made them feel good. Mama couldn't fill this role right now, but God was surrounding her with women who loved her enough to tell her the truth and give her the kick in the pants she needed to stay on track.

"Are we finished with the 'love fest'?" Melba asked. "We've got a wedding in three months. The bride needs to get ready!"

Indigo laughed and flipped through the magazine and brochure and found the invitations she liked best. She pointed to them and passed it to Rachelle for her feedback. It felt good to be thinking about something hopeful for a change.

Yasmin was ever present in her thoughts, though. Wherever she was, she prayed that her sister was safe.

Bring her home, God, and give us a chance to help her reach her goals the right way. Keep her safe, sound, and healthy.

There was always the fear that Yasmin would lapse back into bulimia. Mama and Daddy hadn't voiced that concern, but she knew they were worried. Yasmin might be eighteen and she may have traveled somewhat during her early modeling career, but she was still a green, small-town girl. Only God could keep the predators at bay, and Indigo had to trust that he would.

21

Reuben woke with a start and shuddered.

Not again.

It was three a.m., and he was drenched in sweat. Just like the night before and the night before that, he'd had another bad dream. Same characters, similar scenes, except this time Yasmin was taunting him from afar for not keeping his promise. She blamed him for her missteps.

He glanced at Peyton. The rhythmic rising and falling of her rib cage indicated that for once, she had slept through his drama. Good. One of them needed to get a full night's rest. The dreams had returned full force since Yasmin ran away over a week ago.

Tonight, however, he was struggling against more than his routine nightmare. Reuben couldn't catch his breath, his hands felt clammy, and his heart raced. The fear that he was dying threatened to overwhelm him, but he stayed as calm as he could by reassuring himself that the feeling would pass in a few minutes.

He couldn't believe he was having a panic attack. Not again; not now. The move back to Jubilant was supposed to have cured this.

Reuben sat up straight and sucked in as much air as he could. He had to get out of here.

He swung his feet over the side of the bed and padded across the carpeted floor to his armchair, where he had tossed the pair of jeans he put on after work yesterday. He slid into them and pulled a T-shirt from the laundry basket he had left unattended at the foot of the bed. If he didn't get some air, he might pass out.

He grabbed a pair of sneakers and padded down the stairs, where he sat at the bottom and tucked his feet into the shoes.

Reuben didn't know where he was going, but he needed to clear his head. He strode through the kitchen and opened the door leading to the garage, where he slid behind the wheel of his SUV and pressed the remote to raise the garage door.

Ninety minutes later, by the time he had driven from one end of Jubilant to the other, his heart rate had returned to normal and his chest no longer felt tight. But Reuben still didn't want to go home. Driving calmed him, even as memories of the nightmare lingered.

He was amazed at how quiet and dark the city was. In Seattle, a few pockets of the city would be abuzz with activity even in the wee hours of the morning. The whole town of Jubilant seemed to be sleeping, with the exception of an all-night gas station or convenience store here or there.

When he had run out of places to cruise, Reuben pulled into the parking lot of one of those stores and laid his head on the steering wheel. He wished he could shut off the memories, but after a dream, they replayed in his mind repeatedly, like a video that constantly looped back to the beginning. He wanted to yell or cry or pound his head until the images stopped.

He raised his eyes and peered into the store. The next best thing would be to numb himself. That would have to do.

Reuben climbed out of the Acura and approached the door to the convenience store. Beer. Wine. Whatever. He needed something to make the dream fade. His thoughts turned to Mama and how he'd detested her retreats to her sewing room or to her bedroom, where he knew she was drinking away her sorrows or purposely clouding her memories.

How can I be doing the same?

He'd own up to being a hypocrite tomorrow; right now, he wanted the pain to stop.

Reuben yanked the door to the store, expecting it to open. Instead, it rattled.

The clerk behind the counter waved him away. "We closed five minutes ago!" he yelled and pointed to a clock on the wall that Reuben couldn't see.

"What the—" Reuben felt like punching a hole through the glass. Not because he really needed, or even wanted, a drink; he just wanted some relief.

He climbed back into the SUV and laid his head back on the headrest. He sat there, boring a hole through the windshield with his eyes, trying to remember when he'd last been happy, before the dreams started.

They had become a part of his existence soon after he left Jubilant for college, usually occurring whenever he mentioned the car accident and his upbringing to a friend who sought to know him better.

Tonight, he recalled being visited by police at the hospital after the accident. He remembered being surprised at seeing both sets of his grandparents, who lived out of state. Though he'd only suffered a broken arm and minor scrapes and bruises, he had been admitted for observation to make extra sure he hadn't sustained internal injuries.

The police and his grandparents begged him for information. They wanted to know what had happened, how Dad David had lost control of the van on a quiet stretch of Louisiana highway on a clear day. Reuben didn't have answers. All he remembered was that while he and Mom were singing, everything suddenly went black.

While he lay in that hospital bed for several days, channel surfing and trying to get his bearings, he stumbled upon several TV news reports about the accident. The anchors shared details with the general public that, twenty years later, Mama and Daddy still hadn't discussed with him.

Authorities determined that one of the tires on the Burnses' van blew out, causing David Burns to lose control. Police told news reporters that it was Reuben's desperate screams for his mother to live that had helped authorities find the family and their van in the sloping field, after a truck driver reported spotting broken railing and fresh skid marks in an area he had traveled just hours earlier.

Reuben remembered his grandparents and the hospital chaplain proclaiming that his survival was a gift from God, a sign that he had more living to do. If that were the case, why had he felt so dead inside ever since?

He had come alive when he first went to college in Dallas and realized he could reinvent himself, outside of being known as the courageous orphan survivor, or the child/grandchild of the ultra-holy Charles and Irene Burns. Another vibrant period had been meeting Peyton, whose passion for life and self-confidence pierced his heart. Her blindness didn't intimidate him, and it hadn't taken him long to fall for her. When Charles David was born, he finally understood the meaning of unconditional love. Life had been a joy.

Between those high periods, however, painful memories and guilt over broken promises ebbed and flowed.

Peyton kept urging him to talk to a therapist. Maybe she was right.

Reuben's eyes widened at the sound of rapping on the passenger window. The overly tanned, plump face of the convenience store clerk was almost pressed against the window. Reuben peered into his gray eyes.

He glanced at the store and realized the man had dimmed the lights in the building and was heading to his car. Reuben lowered the window just enough to hear what the man had to say.

"Sorry I couldn't let you in, sir, but I had already closed out the register for the night," he said, and tried to study Reuben's eyes.

Reuben shifted his gaze and nodded. "That's okay, I'll live."

But the man didn't leave. "Sir?"

Reuben was getting annoyed. He wished he had driven off after realizing he couldn't go in. "Yes?" His reply was more of a warning than a question.

"Forgive me if I'm being too forward, but it appears that you're searching for something."

Reuben looked at the man and frowned. He appeared normal, but what was he talking about? Was this question a set up for a robbery or carjacking? Reuben sat up straighter in his seat and glared at the man.

The man raised his palms. "I'm not trying to cause trouble or start anything, I was just asking, because you seem to be in a crisis. I just wanted to suggest that you try prayer. Whatever it is, God can fix it. Really. And if you want, I'll pray for you right now."

Reuben was stunned. A stranger offering to pray for him, early in the morning, when he should be at home? He started the car and put it in reverse. The man backed away when the SUV began to move. Reuben slowly pulled out of the parking spot, then paused to show some respect.

"I need to get home, but thanks anyway," he called to the cashier through the open window. "Send up a prayer in my absence. For the man with the waking nightmares."

The clerk stood in the parking lot and gave Reuben a thumbs-up. "Gotcha," he called out, his voice wafting through the windows. "God can fix that better than anything in the store would have!"

For the first time, Reuben decided he just might believe that.

Ten minutes later, he pulled into his driveway and his heart lurched. Peyton stood in the doorway, with the cordless phone attached to her ears. Tears crisscrossed down her cheeks.

Please, God, no. Don't let anything horrible have happened to Yasmin.

He put the Acura in park and leapt from behind the driver's seat, without bothering to take his keys or lock the door. When he reached Peyton, she was trembling. He'd never seen her so frightened in all the years he'd known her.

He opened the glass storm door and took her into his arms.

"I heard a car, I prayed it was you!" she sobbed into his chest.

"What is it, babe? What happened?"

Peyton pulled away from him and turned her face toward him. "I woke up and you weren't here. I couldn't find you anywhere. I kept calling your cell phone and there was no answer. It's turned off, but it's not in the spot where you usually keep it."

Reuben frowned, trying to remember where he might have put it. In the midst of the panic attack he knew he hadn't taken it with him.

"I knew you'd had another nightmare," Peyton said. "I thought you'd gone and hurt yourself. Don't ever do that to me again, Reuben! That little boy sleeping in there and I need you. We need you!"

She stepped away from him. Reuben reached for her arm and drew her close again.

"I'm sorry babe, I'm so sorry," he said and held her. This time she didn't resist. She clung to him.

It struck him that she'd been strong all these years because she knew he couldn't be. She'd been trying to be brave enough for the both of them; but tonight, when he had left without a word and without being reachable by cell phone, the fragile balance had tipped.

Reuben held her until her sobs quieted and accepted the truth she'd been nudging him to embrace all along. This was about more than him, and a bigger problem than he could handle alone. He needed some help to get through this, or he'd never heal.

22

Max had orchestrated this dinner, and Indigo was still trying to guess his motive.

He knew she had somewhat reconciled with Reuben—her brother was still in their wedding and she wasn't complaining—so what was this about? She asked him again, just before Reuben and Peyton arrived, to no avail.

"Just enjoy yourself, okay?" Max said. "Will that be so hard?"

She and Max and Reuben and Peyton now sat across the table from each other in Max's kitchen, finishing their second helpings of tonight's meal. Taryn had just called to report that Charles David was fine. He was spending the night with her at her parents' house, and she had invited a neighbor's four-year-old son whom she regularly babysat to sleep over too. The boys were preparing for a pillow fight.

"I doubt those boys are eating half as well as we are," Reuben said.

Max had grilled catfish and shrimp. Indigo had prepared rice pilaf, green beans, corn on the cob, and a tossed salad.

"I didn't know professional photographers could burn like this," Reuben said and laughed.

Peyton nudged her husband. "What he meant to say was,

'Thanks to such fabulous hosts for such a fabulous dinner,'" she said. "This was great, you guys. I'm glad we've found some time to get together."

Reuben grew sober and looked pointedly at Indigo. "Yeah, me too," he said. "It means a lot, especially with all that's gone on recently."

Indigo shifted her gaze from Reuben's. She rose from the table and headed toward the island to retrieve dessert. "Do you guys want ice cream with your peach cobbler, or either dessert by itself?"

Peyton patted her hips. "I don't need anything, girlfriend! Living in the South is catching up with me! You guys cook too well and too often! I take Charles David on a daily walk through the neighborhood, but I'm going to have to invest in a treadmill."

Indigo laughed and scooped mint chocolate chip ice cream into a small dish, which she placed in front of Peyton. "Go on, with your tiny self. I heard this is your favorite flavor. I didn't give you too much."

Peyton wagged her finger at Indigo and frowned. "I'm going to pay you back for this, you know." She took a bite and looked at Reuben. "Don't you start complaining when there's more of me to love. It's your sister's fault."

"It's all good, babe," Reuben said.

Indigo smiled as she watched how he gazed at and addressed his wife. It softened her heart toward him some. She had her issues with him, but he was a good guy. Everything she'd seen and heard since he moved back home pointed to that; she just needed to follow everyone's advice and give him a chance. Maybe that was Max's plan all along. Tonight was a good start.

"How'd you two meet?" Max asked Reuben and Peyton. He dug into the bowl of peach cobbler topped with vanilla ice cream that Indigo sat in front of him and Reuben at the same time.

Reuben looked at Peyton. "You want to do the honors?"

"I'm enjoying my ice cream," she said and laughed. "You go ahead!"

Indigo had heard the story before, when Reuben brought Peyton and Charles David home for the first time, four years ago. Mama and Daddy hadn't known how to interact with a blind daughter-in-law who was also the mother of an infant, but Peyton had quickly put them at ease, reassuring them that while they had the advantage of checking her out physically and watching her every move, she would get to know their voices, their footsteps, and more importantly, their hearts, in no time at all. Within days, she had won them over.

It had taken them awhile to give up some of the stereotypical behavior people with disabilities routinely faced—the raised voices when they talked to her, the efforts to hold her hand instead of letting her feel her way around a room and permanently learn how to navigate it. Once they got used to her level of self-sufficiency, her blindness mostly became a non-issue.

Like her routine neighborhood walks with Charles David. Indigo realized she hadn't flinched when Peyton mentioned it, because she knew her sister-in-law had somehow worked out a system with Charles David and with her neighbors that kept both of them safe.

Reuben launched into the tale of their meeting while Max sat back to eat and listen. "I took a break from work one morning to go to the local courthouse and get a copy of the deed to my townhouse, because I was thinking about refinancing," he said. "I was trotting up a set of steep steps when I heard someone call out, 'Excuse me, sir, can you tell me which one of the buildings in this block is the courthouse?'"

Reuben had assumed a high-pitched, singsong voice in the effort to mimic his wife. Peyton swatted his arm.

"Drop the impersonation, please!"

Reuben ignored her and continued. "Well, we were clearly right in front of the courthouse, in front of a big sign at the top of the steps that said as much." He laughed. "I turned around, armed with my sarcastic reply, and there was this tiny woman peering in my direction and carrying a white cane. She was wearing a fitted black pantsuit and had an oversized Coach bag slung over her shoulder, and looked like she'd just stepped off the pages of a fashion magazine.

"Between wondering how she had dressed herself so well and who had dropped her off in downtown Seattle with no instructions, I went back down the steps and offered to lead her up.

"She put me in my place: 'No thank you, I can get up the steps just fine. I simply need to know which building. But thank you.'

"Well, after that, I was intrigued," Reuben said and looked toward Peyton. "First of all, how had she known I was a man if she couldn't see? She had referred to me as 'sir' when she first called out. And how on earth was she getting around Seattle with just a cane, and what could she possibly do in the courthouse without being able to read the records without assistance?

"So I followed her inside and watched her head toward the criminal courts. Well, I knew sight-impaired individuals had a keen sense of hearing, but this girl was amazing. She turned and asked why I was following her, and wanted to know if I needed help."

Reuben laughed at the memory. Peyton swallowed a mouthful of ice cream and grinned.

"I've had limited eyesight since birth and became totally blind when I was three, because of a rare form of hereditary blindness called LCA," she said. "Since I couldn't see well, and eventually not at all, my other senses were heightened. I knew Reuben was a man by the cadence of his walk and the cologne he wore, and for those same reasons, I could tell he was following me once we got inside the courthouse."

Indigo was floored again, just as she had been the first time she'd heard the story. She recalled how she had grieved when she learned she had glaucoma at age twenty-two and how she feared she might someday be blind. Peyton defied what it meant to be sight impaired. She had the most confident and independent spirit of anyone Indigo had met.

Reuben continued. "I told her I was following her because she was beautiful, and I was curious."

Peyton chuckled. "I couldn't see him, but the brother sounded fine. So I bought the line."

Both couples laughed.

"I *did* think she was beautiful," Reuben said. "Look at her—she *is*."

Indigo smiled. Peyton was pretty. With her shoulder-length locks, long eyelashes, heart-shaped face, and cocoa skin, she was a petite Barbie doll. Her sweet and giving spirit made her even more attractive.

Indigo marveled at the fact that her brother hadn't been daunted by Peyton's blindness. That would have been a huge barrier for most men. Reuben obviously had been questioned about that.

"And no," he said, as if reading Indigo's thoughts, "I wasn't intimidated by the fact that she was blind. I think because she was so sure of herself, her lack of sight seemed unimportant. This was a sister who could get where she wanted to go and who was perceptive enough to know who was in her space. That was pretty attractive."

"Well, how did you find out what he looked like?" Max asked Peyton. "I mean, on a first date, do you touch a guy's face to determine his features?"

"I did with Reuben," Peyton said. "After that courthouse encounter, where I was rushing to serve jury duty, he invited me for coffee the next morning. When we met at Starbucks, we just hit it off. We liked the same music, we both got a kick out of betting on how many days of sunshine we'd get each month in Seattle, we had the same philosophy about education and arts, and we enjoyed some of the same hangouts, even though we'd never crossed paths.

"It just seemed like we had been friends forever," Peyton said. "So when he walked me back to the Metro bus stop that morning, I asked if he'd mind if I traced his face with my fingers, to get a sense of who he was.

"Now mind you, we were in a busy area, in the middle of the morning, with other people bustling around us. I was probably already drawing attention because of my shades on a cloudy Seattle day and my white cane. But Reuben Burns said, 'Sure. Help yourself.'

"Because I'm just five feet two, he sat on a bench next to me and turned his face toward me. He let me trace from his forehead to his jaw with both my fingers, right then and there."

Indigo was stunned. This man was her brother, but she really didn't know him.

"Were people watching?" she asked Reuben.

He nodded. "There were quite a few stares. I wasn't embarrassed, but it was a little bit uncomfortable. I liked her though—a lot, and I didn't think it was fair that I knew what she looked like and she didn't have the same goods on me. I survived."

"Well, what'd you think?" Indigo asked.

"My fingers didn't disappoint me—he was handsome!" Peyton said and laughed. "I had to think about future kids, you know?"

Peyton rested a hand on Reuben's arm and sat back and smiled.

"God and I have a pretty good friendship. I talk to him about everything, all the time. I trust that things that happen in my life happen for a reason and usually work out for my good.

"On the morning I had jury duty, a cab was supposed to pick me up and get me to the courthouse early, but the taxi driver had a flat, and the replacement driver was forty minutes away. My parents also lived about half an hour from me at that time. I had just moved into an apartment close to the school where I served as a teacher's assistant while I worked on my master's in education. Mom and Daddy would have gotten me there late too because of the morning commuter traffic." Peyton leaned forward and made a teepee with her hands as she continued down memory lane.

"So I did the next best thing and called ACCESS, a private transportation company that takes disabled residents wherever they need to go throughout the Seattle area. By the time they dropped me off downtown, I had ten minutes to spare before court started.

"I told the driver to let me out and I'd find my way inside. That's when I heard Reuben running up a set of steps. Had my taxi been on time, that never would have happened. Not everyone I meet feels comfortable offering me help. Reuben not only was comfortable, he also had the nerve to flirt with me!

"Then, when he asked for a coffee date and allowed me to trace his face in public?" Peyton slapped the table with the palm of her hand. "That was it. I knew that God had sent my soul mate. I just had to wait for him to tell Reuben."

Reuben squirmed in his seat and Peyton patted his arm.

"He doesn't talk to God like I do, didn't then and still doesn't now, but God worked it all out," she said.

Indigo was curious about that last comment. As much as Christians made about not being unequally "yoked," or marrying someone who wasn't at the same level of faith, how had Peyton determined that Reuben still fit the bill if he were missing that criteria? She'd have to ask her that later.

Reuben resumed the story. "I don't know if I knew that day that she would be my wife, but I knew I had found someone special. There was just something about her. She was more independent and more focused than any other woman I had met, and yet she had this soft side—she wasn't afraid to still be a woman and allow me to wine and dine her and open doors for her. I probably knew she was the one by the third date."

"But—" Peyton held up a finger and smirked. "He already had a girlfriend, and she wasn't too happy when he started backing off, especially when she found out it was for a 'handicapped chick,' as she unkindly put it."

"Ya'll had some drama!" Indigo said and laughed. "Peyton, did you beat her down or pray for her?"

Peyton laughed. "Neither. I didn't have the problem—either she did or Reuben did. They needed to decide individually and as a couple what they were going to do. In the meantime, I just kept being me and doing my thing. If Reuben wanted to go out, fine. If he didn't call, fine. I stayed focused on my graduate classes, my young students, and on taking care of me. That's why I was always so cute when he saw me!"

Max grinned at Indigo and took her hand.

"You sound a little like my babe," Max told Peyton. "When I first tried to date her, she kept putting me off, because she had just ended an engagement. She was doing her own thing in New York, and I had to convince her that I was her guy."

Reuben nodded. "They are alike, man," he said. "I'd call Peyton to ask for a date and she'd tell me I should have called earlier in the week—she had plans. I'd offer to take her places and she'd refuse, determined to rely on her regular modes of transportation because she didn't use friends that way.

"It wasn't until I made up my mind that she was the one, that things got better," he said and laughed. "I officially ended it with the other girl and told Peyton that I needed her to give me a chance."

Peyton blushed. "He said I made him better, just by being me. Isn't that why we give ourselves to someone else in a relationship? Not just for our own needs, but to help them thrive and become all they can be?

"We were leaving dinner one night when he shared that, and I was done. He had me. When he proposed after just six months, I said yes."

They kissed lightly now and smiled at each other. Peyton obviously couldn't see Reuben's reaction, but she seemed to innately know it was there.

"How long have you two been married? Any pointers for us?" Max asked.

"Six years," Reuben said.

Indigo again wondered how he could have done that without letting Mama and Daddy know.

"Did you have a wedding?" she asked. Caution filled Reuben's eyes when he nodded and she knew he'd heard the edge in her voice.

"Yeah, we did," he said. "In the church that Peyton attended her entire life." He hesitated, but continued. "It was beautiful."

Indigo couldn't help herself, despite the warning in Max's eyes. She felt herself growing angry again, but maybe Reuben could temper her fire with his answer.

"Who sat on the groom's side of the church? What did you tell Peyton about your family?"

Reuben reached for Peyton's hand. Before he could respond, she did.

"He told me the truth, Indigo," she said.

"Which was?"

Peyton cocked her ear toward Reuben and waited.

"I told her that my parents were dead and that my paternal grandparents who raised me lived in Texas and I hadn't seen them in years. I told her I had two sisters that I hadn't been as close to as I should have, and I would feel awkward inviting you guys to my wedding when I had been out of touch for so long. I told her that I loved her and wanted to build a life with her, but I was still trying to figure out what do with my old life."

It seemed odd to Indigo that a girl who was as self-assured as Peyton had been described would fall for someone as ambivalent as Reuben made himself sound. There had to be more to this story. If there weren't, he was as selfish as she had imagined all this time.

"When did you figure out 'what to do with your old life,' Reuben?" Indigo asked. "Or better yet, what led you to finally give up the good life and come back here? Were you running from something?"

Max squeezed her knee under the table, letting her know she had overstepped her brother's boundaries.

"I'm still figuring out what to do with my past, Indigo," he said and peered into her eyes. "Truthfully, that's why I came back home. The fact that Yasmin has run away breaks my heart, because getting closer to you two is part of that plan. I'm not running away from anything, I'm running toward something, I hope."

He looked at Peyton before continuing. "I hope you and I can work through whatever animosity you have toward me, Indigo, so we can be there for each other. That's what I want. That's what I'm struggling for."

Indigo folded her arms across her chest. His choice of the word "struggling" puzzled her. What did that mean?

"Really, Reuben? What else do you want? Me to forget that when I was fourteen you went off to college and left me at home to deal with Mama's alcoholism and Daddy's emotional absence, and a little sister who was needy and had no one but me? You want me to forget that you rarely called and you never checked on me? When you left for college and refused to come back, you didn't just leave Mama and Daddy behind, you left me and you left Yasmin. She was too young to really have a connection, but I needed you, Reuben. I really did."

She hadn't meant to go there, but the truth poured out before she could stop herself. Tears teetered on her lids and her voice quivered. It felt good to release her frustrations, but she knew she had opened up a set of new issues with her brother.

"I'm sorry," she said once she had composed herself. "I'm out of line. I should have saved all of that for another time." She should have saved it for the leather journal she'd been pouring her heart into lately, she chided herself.

Reuben's smile was rueful. "I'm glad you didn't, Indigo. Until everyone in this family starts owning their issues and accepting that we can't control each other's choices and perspectives, someone's always going to feel trapped, like they're living a lie just to keep the peace. We're not going to get Yasmin home until we change that and start loving each other unconditionally."

Indigo couldn't mask her surprise. Reuben kept countering her judgment of him with just what she needed to hear.

It struck her, as she recognized the sincerity in his voice and for the first time saw the pain that filled his eyes, that while she had been condemning him for his past, he had been judging himself by that same measure.

She was still angry at the college-bound brother who left Jubilant thirteen years earlier, but tonight she'd had dinner and fellowship with the man he had become. This person was someone special, someone to be admired. She had to find a way to accept that and stop harping on the past.

If she didn't, she would be no better than the old Reuben or the young Yasmin. She hadn't estranged herself from the family to figure out who she was, but she had been clinging so tightly to her expectations of everyone else's role that she was in danger of repeating the crippling patterns that had kept the Burnses from growing and thriving.

Indigo decided right then that she didn't want to take those issues into her marriage with Max. She wanted better for herself and for her future children, and she was willing to do whatever it would take to change.

She looked at Max and saw that he recognized her "lightbulb moment."

He had been trying to tell her this all along. Thank God for sending her a man who was patient enough to hang in there until she got it.

23

Reuben was surprised at how quickly he and Peyton had grown to enjoy the laidback, slower pace of life in Jubilant, but church remained his least favorite place.

Yet, here he was on a Wednesday evening, driving to Bible study at St. Peter's Baptist. He let Peyton talk him into coming because Charles David enjoyed the youth Bible class as much as she enjoyed the women's group.

"Consider this your chance for some guy time," she told him. "You men can bond and talk about God without a bunch of women butting in."

Male bonding? Over God? Just what he looked forward to after a long day at work.

But Reuben knew he needed to compromise. He still hadn't worked up the nerve to find a therapist since he'd left home in the middle of the night two weeks ago, during his panic attack. He was still shaken by the incident, and by Peyton's response to it, but Jubilant was a fishbowl. He had decided he might have to drive to Houston or Austin to seek confidential counseling.

After their dinner with Indigo and Max, though, Peyton had casually suggested that Max might offer the support he needed.

"He's a good guy, rock solid. I think you could trust him," she said more than once.

Reuben actually agreed; but men didn't call each other up professing the need to talk. When an opportunity presented itself, he'd see if Max were open to listening, without feeling caught between him and Indigo.

This evening, he was surprised to see Max's car when he pulled into St. Peter's parking lot. Max attended Wednesday night Bible study? This brother might be too good to be true.

Reuben took the brand-new Bible Peyton handed him without complaining. "It's got my name on it," he said in surprise.

"Yep," she said and unbuckled herself. "I picked it up at the local Christian bookstore and asked them to personalize it. Feel free to write in it and jot down notes from tonight's meeting."

Reuben grew tense. If she had taken the time to go out and buy a Bible, she was intent on making this a weekly habit. Great.

He wouldn't balk for now. Maybe he could schedule the counseling sessions on Wednesday evenings. First, he'd have to find Peyton and Charles David a regular ride to church. The answer came quickly: as much as Mama loved hanging out at his house lately, she was a shoo-in for the job.

Reuben opened the door to the side entrance of St. Peter's and followed his wife and son into the church's education building. Max approached them from the opposite end of the hall, with a camera slung over each shoulder.

He hugged Peyton and Charles David, then clasped hands with Reuben.

"You heading out, man?" Reuben asked. "I thought I was going to have some company in my first Bible study."

Max chuckled. "I guess I should be here on Wednesday nights, but I'm usually working. I'm here tonight taking an official portrait of the pastor, for his upcoming anniversary service." Max paused. "You know what? I don't have plans for the evening. Indigo is working late tonight, processing the photos she took on her trip to London. How about I stay and sit in tonight? They'll be glad to see both of us."

Reuben's pride wanted him to balk, to tell Max to be on his way. But he swallowed it. He would appreciate having Max's company in a setting he knew would make him uncomfortable.

"Thanks, man," he said. "How did things go for Indigo in London? She have a good time?"

Max shrugged. "Yes and no. The job was a wonderful experience, and she made a good impression on the museum officials who hired her," he said. "But she was antsy the whole time, worried that Yasmin might finally reach out to her while she was so far away. I think she was crushed all the more that nothing happened after all—no call, no text, nothing from Yas."

Reuben nodded. He couldn't believe that the baby of the family had disappeared without a trace, without the thoughtfulness to at least check in and let everyone know she was okay.

Fannie Grey, the leader of the women's Bible study, interrupted his reverie when she pranced down the hall toward them. Her name was more fitting for an older woman, yet she was anything but, Reuben mused. In her late thirties, her face was flawlessly made up, her jeans and casual blouse fit her size 6 frame snugly but appropriately, and every inch of her flowing hair was in place.

"Good evening, Burns family!" She bent over and scooped up Charles David in a hug. Her perfume must have been strong; the minute she encircled him with her arms, he had a sneezing attack.

"My goodness!" she said, and pulled back to avoid getting sprayed. Max and Reuben traded glances and stifled their laughs.

Fannie stood back from the little boy and offered to guide Peyton and Charles David to their classes.

"See you in an hour," Peyton said to Reuben. "I'll meet you in this area when we're done."

Max motioned with his head for Reuben to follow him. "I've been to Bible study a few times in the past few months. I'll show you where we meet." He lowered his voice as they strolled down the corridor. "It's not too bad. Pastor Taylor usually leads it, and he really keeps it real."

Several men were arranging folding chairs in a semicircle when Max opened the door to the classroom. Reuben followed him inside.

"Well, hello, fellas!" bellowed an older gentleman, who appeared to be in his sixties. He extended his right hand to Max and then to Reuben.

"I know the young photographer here, and I've seen you in church on occasion," he said to Reuben. "Welcome. I'm Joe Hartley."

"Thanks, nice to meet you," Reuben said.

Another older man, Deacon Painter, approached Reuben and gave him a hug. "Good to see you here, young man. I'm glad you and your family are settling into St. Peter's," he said. "Joe, Reuben Burns was my Sunday school student years ago, before he left for college and started his career in Washington State. This is Charles' boy. He's a good man."

Reuben smiled politely at the introduction and remembered that Daddy would be here tonight too, if his blood pressure weren't elevated. He should have called him to see how he was feeling.

"I moved to Jubilant about ten years ago and joined the church soon after," Joe said. "There's a lot of family history here that I'm still learning. Don't worry, though, this group isn't all gray heads. There are some young cats too. They'll be strolling in soon."

Reuben hoped his relief didn't register on his face. He stepped into the hall to call Daddy on his cell while Max grabbed two seats.

"Hey, Daddy, I forgot to check and see if you and Mama were coming to Bible study tonight. I'm here with Peyton."

"Naw, son, not tonight," Daddy said, sounding more lethargic than usual. He hadn't been himself since Yasmin's disappearance three weeks ago. Reuben noticed he picked up the phone on the first ring every time he called, even though caller ID would have told him if it were Yasmin.

"Is your pressure high?"

"No, today was a good day," Daddy said with a sigh.

"I know things are tough, Daddy. We gotta keep our spirits up, though. Yasmin's going to come around. I just know it."

Daddy didn't answer for what seemed like minutes. "I hope you're right, son. I love that girl, maybe I just didn't show it the right way."

Reuben wanted to tell him to stop beating himself up. He wanted to leave right now and go sit with him, to console him. But Pastor Taylor rounded the corner, with Bible in hand. He grinned when he saw Reuben.

"Daddy, you did the best you could, and you are still doing that," Reuben said quickly. "You're a good father. Bible study is about to start. I'll call you back later tonight, okay?"

He ended the call just as Pastor Taylor approached him for a handshake and a hug.

Reuben was sure the pastor had worn his official robe for the photos Max had just taken, but now he was clad in jeans, a T-shirt that said "Livin' for Christ," and a pair of Air Jordans. He was fifty-five this year, according to Aunt Melba, who styled his wife's hair, but he could pass for at least five years younger.

"Good to see you, Brother Burns! Welcome!"

They entered the classroom together and Pastor Taylor did a double take when he saw Max. "I didn't even guilt you into staying and here you are!"

Both men laughed and slapped palms.

"I've still got a lot to learn," Max said. "I'm glad to be here."

By the time they opened with prayer ten minutes later, the group was a dozen strong, and several men in their twenties and thirties had arrived. Reuben was floored. What was drawing them out on a weeknight?

When Bible study began, he thought he understood. The lessons were biblically based, but relevant.

"Tonight we're reading Isaiah 38," Pastor Taylor told the group. He gave them time to find the passage in their Bibles, and Reuben was relieved to see out of the corner of his eye that he wasn't the only one who needed to check the contents page first.

When he located the appropriate book and chapter, he skimmed it quickly. Pastor Taylor asked Brother Joe to read the first half aloud and Brother Tim, one of the younger men who had joined them, to read the latter half.

When they were done, Pastor Taylor asked the men to share their perceptions of the passage. What had it meant?

"King Hezekiah wanted to live. He begged God to spare his life," one of the men said.

"He was tight with God, so God gave him more time," another offered.

And yet another: "His relationship with God was so good that God allowed him to see what was coming down the pike and gave him a chance to respond."

"All of that is true," Pastor Taylor said, after hearing the varying comments. "Now tell me how this passage applies to your life, about something you're asking God for, or maybe something you've asked him for in the past."

Reuben's heart pounded. He couldn't go there tonight.

All of the men remained quiet, so Pastor Taylor piped up. "My story is fairly dramatic, so I had planned to save it for last, but I'll go first. Like Hezekiah, I made a plea to God, but he didn't seem to answer."

The men sat up straighter or leaned in to hear where Pastor Taylor was going with this.

"I asked God to spare my first wife, Farrah," he said. "We had been married just three years and were planning to start a family. We were living in Wisconsin, and she decided to go on a mission trip to Thailand with a few co-workers from the Christian school where she taught. I was in seminary and working part-time at a homeless shelter, so I couldn't get the time off to join her.

"Three days into what was supposed to be a two-week trip, the group's living quarters were invaded by bandits. A handful of teenagers from the orphanage they were visiting had accompanied Farrah and the other teachers back to their quarters, to try on some donated American clothing. When the women didn't return with the kids in time for dinner, the orphanage director alerted authorities that something was amiss." Pastor Taylor closed his eyes and continued.

"The relatives of the other teachers and I were notified by the American Embassy that the group had been kidnapped and were being held hostage. Embassy officials thought the bandits wanted money. I was struggling to make ends meet and didn't have much, but I was willing to beg or borrow to get my wife home. Of course, the U.S. government didn't want to negotiate with criminals. The other teachers' spouses and parents and I did all we could do: turn to God." Pastor Taylor opened his eyes then, and made eye contact with each man in the circle.

"We held daily prayer vigils, and each of us had our extended family praying around the country. We held press conferences and asked for other Americans to support us however they could to get these five citizens home. We asked God to deliver our relatives, as a sign that he was in control and that he still worked miracles. I believed in my heart that this was absolutely going to happen. Farrah was going to come home and she'd have a powerful testimony to share.

"But a week after the bandits took over the place, we learned that she and the others had been tied up and tossed in a river. These criminals murdered my wife and the others to send America a message that the United States' disdain for the needs of the Thai people would no longer be tolerated. It was all over the news, if any of you were watching and listening about two decades ago."

Pastor Taylor's missionary wife had been murdered? Reuben felt sucker-punched. He could tell that the other men who hadn't heard this story, including Max, were stunned too.

"The Thai government allowed officials from the American Embassy to retrieve the bodies, but the bandits were never caught. I buried my wife and became consumed with anger. I had a crisis of faith after that." Pastor Taylor stared off into space. "Here I was in seminary and I couldn't get a prayer through to God? Something was very wrong with this picture."

He eyed each of the men. "How many of you have found yourself in that spot, in a place where you're trusting God, pleading with God, to make things right, and he seems deaf?"

A few of the older men raised their hands and shook their heads as memories consumed them.

Tim, who had read part of the biblical passage, raised his hand and bowed his head.

Max's hand went up, and Reuben found himself slowly raising his too.

"Were the students killed too, Pastor Taylor?" one of the younger men asked.

Pastor Taylor shook his head. "That's the victory, son. I'm heading there," he said, and resumed his story. "I was heartbroken, just devastated, after Farrah's death. She and I had met during our freshman year of college, dated throughout and waited two years after graduation to get married, so that we could be sure we were ready. We had just bought our first house, a tiny place that Farrah had made as lovely as she could on our limited budget. She was the light there, and in my life. I just didn't think I could go on.

"I took a leave of absence from seminary and went to work full-time for the shelter as the assistant director," Pastor Taylor said. "I'm not really sure I helped anyone in those days, because I was bitter and disillusioned, just going through the motions. And then one Wednesday morning, about a year after I buried Farrah, I arrived home from work and sat in my car, feeling paralyzed." Pastor Taylor looked off into space, as if reliving that day in his mind.

"I just didn't think I could go into that house that still so heavily bore my wife's presence, and not go off on this so-called gracious God. I got out of the car and retrieved my mail, but got back in the car to open and read it, instead of going inside.

"Well, lo and behold, there was a letter there from the director of the orphanage in Thailand, the very place where my Farrah had gone to minister. It was written to me and to the families of the other victims. The director, who happened to be a Christian minister, described how the six students who had been with our relatives during their captivity were returned to the orphanage unharmed, but changed forever.

"During the week they had spent as hostages with our relatives, they saw the women singing worship songs and praises to God. They asked Farrah and the others how they could have such peace when they were in such danger, and the women shared with the kids why they trusted God and would love him no matter what.

"Apparently, this blew the kids' minds. When Farrah and the others were led away to the river, the teenagers were dropped off just outside the orphanage and warned to forget everything they saw and heard. But most of them couldn't forget, and didn't want to.

"The letter shared how, within a year of the incident, all six of them had professed a commitment to serve Christ because of the faith they had witnessed in Farrah and her friends. All of them wanted to work in ministry somehow, whether professionally or as volunteers, wherever they could transform lives.

"When I finished the letter, it all clicked for me." Pastor Taylor brought his hands together. "I wanted God to answer my prayer and let Farrah live. I felt like he had let me down. Instead, I eventually realized that he had used Farrah's life to show a group of impressionable teens how to live. Because of their experience with these teachers who professed a love for Christ and never faltered, those kids began spreading the gospel among their peers—in the orphanage and at school, and wherever life took them, despite the dangers of doing so. I've prayed over the years that all of them are still to this day somewhere giving others hope."

Joe Hartley shook his head. "I don't know, Pastor. That seems like a pretty big sacrifice. I mean, I love your current wife, First Lady Marlayne, but to lose your first wife like that, whew! And what does that have to do with this Scripture? Hezekiah asked God to let him live longer and his wish was granted—he got fifteen more years!"

Pastor Taylor smiled wryly. "There was a time when I felt as you do, Brother Joe. Actually, I still do on some days. But when

I look at this Scripture and consider the fact that God granted Hezekiah's request, I see it as a bonus. Like the unearned grace and mercy we're granted when we mess up or knowingly sin and don't suffer dire consequences.

"God loves us and wants to give us his best, and when we ask in faith and obedience, he usually honors our requests. The key is for us to know what his will is for our lives and to operate inside that purpose.

"Honestly, it's easy to question why a good and just God would let innocent people, who were in a foreign land trying to serve him, be mistreated and murdered. How is that a reward? But because he knows all and sees all, we have to trust that he's maneuvering even where evil exists and working everything out for our good." Pastor Taylor made eye contact with the men again.

"So when we pray, we want to be as earnest and as sincere and as obedient as Hezekiah, but we also want to be inside God's will, at every turn. And that's the true challenge—knowing when he wants us to move and when he wants us to stand still. Knowing when to ask for a miracle and when to accept that what seems like our worst experience can, in God's timing, yield the greatest of victories.

"I can now look back on that season without bitterness. I remember my last conversation with Farrah before she boarded the plane to leave, and how she said, with such clarity, that she was ready to do whatever God required of her. I think that took such courage. I don't know that I had that kind of courage then, or that I do now."

Reuben raised his hand. "How did you find your way back to the ministry?"

If Pastor Taylor could accomplish that feat, it gave him hope that he could find his way into his sisters' hearts.

Pastor Taylor took a breath and folded his arms. "That there is a whole new story, another testimony in and of itself. The short answer is that God had to get my attention, and when he did, I stopped running. I've never regretted turning back to him.

"Now that you know a little more about my journey, tell me, what does the Scripture that we read this evening say to you? Name it and claim it? Be in tune with God and trust him to guide?"

No one broke the silence.

"You see, we bring to this passage our personal histories, our hopes, desires, and dreams, and even our wish lists. But what we need to bring to God is only this simple request: 'Let me live for you.' Because as another Scripture tells us, 'To live is Christ, to die is gain.'

"That means it's better to take the path that Farrah took rather than live a meaningless life of going through the motions and pretending to have it all together. When we allow ourselves to be broken, as Hezekiah was, we can then be blessed. Everyone knew Hezekiah was terminally ill, so when the remedy was applied that allowed him to live, he couldn't help but glorify God in the way he lived going forward.

"Is your life bringing God glory? I had to ask myself that back then, and I do that on a daily basis now. Ask yourself this question, and find the courage to hear God's answer.

"Whew! I done preached up in here!" Pastor Taylor closed his Bible and wiped his brow.

Indeed he had.

Reuben would need to process all of this later, but he wondered if he had been overlooking the answers to the questions he'd been wrestling with all these years. Why did his parents have to die, and why had he survived? Why would a good God let that happen?

He hadn't found any great meaning yet, like Pastor Taylor had so vividly described. He'd just been a kid longing to be held by his parents again, and wondering why his pleas for God to save them had gone unanswered, when his biological mother had always read him the Scripture in Mark that said "Ask and you shall receive."

Tonight was the first inkling he had that maybe God had heard, and maybe their deaths were part of a bigger plan. But what did that mean for him? Was there something more he was being called to do? He didn't think he even liked God; how effective would that make him in spreading the so-called gospel?

24

The call from New York came when she least expected it, and it disappointed her that it wasn't from Yasmin.

Indigo rummaged through her purse to find the ringing cell phone and had gasped when she saw the 212 area code. New York City.

She didn't recognize the number, but that could mean that Yasmin was calling from someone else's phone.

She winced and looked at Max. "It could have been her. I just missed it."

The phone chimed a second later, though, letting her know she had a new voice mail. Indigo breathlessly checked it, hoping to hear her sister's voice.

Her face fell as she listened. It wasn't Yasmin, but the message still surprised her. It was from Sasha Davies, the talent scout for Ford Models who had signed Yasmin four years ago. Why would Sasha be calling her? She hadn't hired Indigo for a fashion photo shoot since Mama and Daddy yanked Yasmin out of the business.

"Indigo, give me a call as soon as you can. I need to talk with you about . . . an opportunity. Please call ASAP."

"That was strange," Indigo told Max when the call ended.

It was Saturday afternoon, and they were driving through some of the newer neighborhoods sprouting up in Jubilant, looking for a house they could grow into, yet comfortably afford, on their fluctuating entrepreneurial income. So far they'd stopped at two open houses for older homes that were fairly spacious, but lacked curb appeal. As visual professionals, loving the look was important to both of them.

"Who was it?" Max asked.

"Yasmin's former boss, from her modeling days. She used to hire me to shoot portfolio images of some of her new recruits, and for an occasional low-profile show, but I haven't heard from her since Yas stopped modeling. Isn't it funny that she'd call now?"

Max looked at her pointedly. "Maybe not, babe. She may know something."

Indigo frowned. "Think so? I don't recall her and Yasmin being particularly tight. But you know what? You're right—you never know how things work out."

She dialed Sasha back and got her voice mail.

"Sasha—great to hear from you. This is Indigo Burns, returning your call. Please call me back at your convenience. I'm looking forward to talking with you."

Indigo sighed and placed the phone on top of her bag, so if it rang again, she could easily grab it. On impulse, she picked it up again and dialed Yasmin's cell number. As it had been doing since the girl's birthday a month ago, the call went straight to voice mail. Yasmin was smart: if she had a phone now, it must be one of the pay-as-you-go kind, that you could cheaply add minutes to, without being traced.

But for her not to have contacted anyone was alarming. And unfair. She knew Mama and Daddy were older, and that Daddy had high blood pressure. The stress of worrying about her wasn't good for either of them. They didn't deserve to be treated this way.

Indigo laid the phone down again and picked up the newspaper's real estate section.

"Make a left here," she told Max.

They turned onto a tree-lined street with wide sidewalks and lush lawns. The two-story brick homes weren't all cookie-cutter designs. Moms were pushing babies in strollers and kids wore helmets and raced on their bikes in a couple of the cul-de-sacs they passed. When they pulled in front of the house listed for sale, Indigo was smitten.

She looked at Max with wide eyes.

He smirked. "Don't fall in love curbside. Let's look inside first."

Indigo wasn't disappointed. The first floor featured wood floors, a large kitchen with a bar and island, surround sound already installed, and a sliding glass door that led to a backyard stone patio. Upstairs, there were four bedrooms, a theater room, and a walk-up attic with a small bonus room.

Indigo and Max nodded in unison.

"Big enough for an on-site office," he said.

There was nothing to dislike, as far as Indigo was concerned. This house was beautiful from the inside out and gave them plenty of room to grow. They could use one of the second-floor bedrooms as an additional office until they added to their family. The neighborhood schools were fantastic, which would keep the property value elevated, and it was just fifteen or so minutes from Max's studio in one direction and her parents' home in the other.

They stood on the second-floor landing, peering past the elaborate chandelier at the cherrywood floor below. The realtor who was based in the neighborhood to show this home and others had stepped outside to take a call.

Max grasped Indigo by the waist and twirled her around several times. She leaned in for a kiss.

“What do you think?” she whispered as she nuzzled his neck with her nose.

“It’s off the chain, but it’s over our budget,” he whispered back and kissed her chin.

Indigo pulled away from him and peered into his eyes. “How do you know? Did you get the asking price?”

Max shook his head. “No, but I’m guessing it’s way up there.”

Indigo wasn’t going to argue with him. She didn’t want to make him feel bad if he were right and they were out of their league. But she also didn’t want to give up without trying. She felt at home here, and she believed he did too.

When the realtor returned and climbed the steps to join them, Max popped the question.

“What’s the asking price?”

Ms. Jaynes quoted a figure well above what Indigo and Max considered comfortable, given their current income.

Her heart fell, but she wasn’t ready to give up just yet. “What kind of programs do you have for first-time home buyers?”

Max chimed in too. “Actually, she’s a first-time buyer, but I’d be willing to sell my current house and put those proceeds toward this down payment.”

Ms. Jaynes motioned for them to follow her. “Let’s go to my office down the block. We’ll see what’s doable through a variety of options.”

Max and Indigo looked at each other and smiled. She decided in that instant that whatever was wisest would be okay, even if it meant crossing this fabulous home off her list. They were just starting out and didn’t have to have it right away; what was more important was being together, wherever they lived.

Max’s cell phone rang when they hopped into his SUV to follow the realtor to her office.

"Hey, man," he said and mouthed to Indigo that it was Reuben. It intrigued her to see them bonding, but she hadn't balked. After their dinner a couple of weeks ago, she had realized that God was going to reveal everything she needed to know about Reuben's long absence, to give her some resolution. It would happen in God's timing, not hers. She just had to wait and be obedient.

Maybe that was why Reuben called at this precise moment; to remind her about that instruction even as she was house hunting.

Max made plans to get together with Reuben later that evening, to shoot pool. She made a mental note to give Peyton a call. Maybe they could hang out too.

25

Peyton answered Indigo's call through the voice-automated speakerphone in her family room and agreed to visit with Indigo while the men played pool.

She also offered to bring dinner.

Indigo dismissed the idea. "I invite you over and make you do the work? I don't think so, lady."

"It won't take but a minute to whip up my chicken tetrazzini. You'll love it. You helped cook last time, remember?"

"That was at Max's place," Indigo said and laughed.

"Counts as yours informally," Peyton said. "It won't be long 'til that 'yours' and 'mine' stuff officially becomes 'ours.'"

Indigo shook her head. "It's sneaking up on me. I can't believe it."

"Have you mailed your invitations yet?"

"They'll go out in two more weeks."

The women chatted a few minutes more before Peyton ended the call so she could wake Charles David from his nap to get him ready for the visit.

Indigo began tidying up her townhouse, but soon stopped in her tracks and laughed out loud. Peyton was blind; girlfriend couldn't see dust and piles of books and photography magazines.

She resumed the task, though, because Charles David could. Plus, she knew Peyton could feel and sense her way around a space. Somehow she'd know if the rooms were cluttered.

Half an hour later, Reuben called to tell her they were pulling into the driveway. Peyton used her cane to approach the front door, and Indigo greeted her from her townhouse's tiny porch landing. She leaned down to hug Peyton and peered around her.

"Someone's missing. Where's Charles David?"

"He wanted to go over to Irene's and play on his swing set. I think your mother bribed him with ice cream too," Peyton shook her head. "She is spoiling that boy rotten and there's nothing I can do about it."

Indigo knew Mama was trying to fill the void left by Yasmin's absence. Despite her efforts to replace her fretting for Yas with adoration for Charles David, she was suffering. She seemed to have aged at least five years, and her spirits were as low as Daddy's. They were becoming two hermits who came to life only when Charles David was around to help take their minds off their woes. Mama seemed to have completely forgotten about the wedding, and Indigo hadn't had the heart to bother her. It hurt, though, to lose her sister and her mother in one fell swoop.

The journaling that Rachelle had recommended was helping. Pouring out her thoughts and feelings on paper every night, especially after a trying day at work or an emotionally draining one with the family, was helping her keep her equilibrium.

She didn't spend as much time crying about her problems to God, either. He already knew about them. Her time with him these days was mostly spent in meditation, listening for direction on the path he wanted her to take.

Peyton made her way into Indigo's living room and tucked her cane into her purse before settling on the sofa. "Mind if I take off my shoes? This sofa is comfortable, and I just might curl up on it for a while, since I'm on my own little 'play date' of sorts, away from the men in my life."

Indigo laughed. She loved this girl's spirit. She curled up on the opposite end of the couch and the two of them chitchatted about whatever crossed their minds—the lack of social outlets for women their age in Jubilant, the latest dramas among the Hollywood elite, and who should have won last season's *American Idol* competition.

Eventually they grew hungry and moved to the table to feast on Peyton's tetrazzini, which included spaghetti pasta, shredded chicken, and mozzarella cheese.

"This is sinful!" Indigo said as she dished up her second serving. "How did you learn how to throw down like this?"

Peyton laughed. "I don't have to be a girl raised in the South to know how to cook. I've been burnin' forever. That's how I got your brother."

They both had a good laugh.

"Seriously, though," Peyton said. "I'm the youngest of three girls, and when I was born with limited vision and eventually became blind, my parents decided they were going to raise me as much like they had raised my sisters as they could.

"Phaedra and Paula learned to ride their bikes when they were six, so when I turned ten and my legs were long enough, my parents bought a two-seater bike that allowed me to learn to ride as the 'passenger.' My sisters sorted their laundry to be washed starting at age ten and then folded it afterward, and I did the same. Both of them learned to cook at age twelve, so when I turned twelve, Mom got whatever adaptive equipment she needed so she could teach me too. It turns out that I'm the best cook of the three."

Indigo was floored. "Is there anybody else in your immediate family who's blind?"

"No. Both of my parents carry the recessive gene for this condition, but it's fairly rare. One of my father's aunts was born with LCA, but because of her age and the era in which she lived, she had a limited life and was mostly confined to a home. My dad was determined to help me become independent, so that when he and Mom were gone, I wouldn't be left at anyone else's mercy. I thank God that he and Mom were so focused on helping me be strong."

"They sound amazing," Indigo said. "You *are* amazing, and I guess it stems from having their support. I really admire you."

"Please, Indigo, no fan-club fawning, okay?" Peyton reached for her hand. Indigo rested her palm inside of Peyton's open one. "Let's keep it real, okay? I haven't always been this strong or this accepting of my condition. I had a really rough time when I was a teenager, because I couldn't understand why I was 'marked,' why I had to be the 'black sheep' of the family. I thought about suicide."

Indigo gasped. Looking at Peyton, watching her in action with Reuben and Charles David, and seeing that bright, cheerful smile, one never would have guessed.

"I did," Peyton nodded. "But I had a really good girlfriend who accepted me unconditionally and loved me for me. She always took me to church with her family, and one Sunday, there was a guest minister, a college student, who preached about taking the blinders off, about the importance of taking the scales off our eyes so we could really see what God wanted us to see.

"That helped me so much. I realized that just because I couldn't see with my physical eyes didn't mean I couldn't see spiritually, with the heart of God. The only thing that was crippled was my mind. I gave my life to Christ that day, and even though I occasionally struggled with self-pity and depression for a few more years, God kept making me stronger, until I woke up one day and realized that there was a whole lot more of me to love than there was to hate."

Indigo wrapped her fingers around Peyton's hand and gave it a squeeze. She thought about her own pity party over her glaucoma diagnosis and how Daddy had nudged her out of her self-absorption by directing her to run Melba's hair salon, until Aunt Melba recovered from her stroke. By taking her eyes off of herself, she had wound up receiving everything she needed to thrive, including winning a photography award and meeting Max. In her own way, Peyton had traveled a similar path.

"I'm so glad you finally saw the truth," Indigo told her. "I'm thankful that you're my sister-in-law."

"Even though you don't like your brother?"

Peyton reminded Indigo of Aunt Melba; she wasn't one to dilly-dally around the elephant in the room. Indigo wasn't sure how to respond.

Peyton nodded. "I know. It's been hard. I heard you at dinner a couple of weeks ago, when you vented your frustrations. Just know that Reuben hasn't been as self-absorbed as you think. He's been wrestling with his own demons from the past."

Indigo frowned. "What do you mean?"

Peyton pursed her lips. "It's not my place to share that. He'll talk to you when he's ready. I've been praying for God to get him there, and he will."

Indigo's curiosity was piqued. It was clear that she'd been assessing her brother on partial information, but Peyton wasn't going to talk.

"Well, tell me this," Indigo said, changing courses. "How is it that someone so deeply connected to her faith fell in love with a man who barely knows how to say grace? You've met Mama and Daddy, so you know Reuben grew up in church. But it's been clear since he came back home that he'd rather run through fire than call on the Lord."

Peyton's smile exuded sadness. "It's tough to see him estranged from God, isn't it?"

Indigo's heart went out to her sister-in-law. "How did you get past that and decide to marry him, since God has been so important to you for so long? It's almost like you went against biblical teachings."

"The thing is, those 'teachings' are open to interpretation," Peyton said. "That's why it's so important to have a connection with God for yourself, so you can understand what he wants you to specifically glean from his Word. What he speaks to *you* through the Scriptures might be different from the message he has for me. That's why we're each accountable to him for our actions, our words, and our deeds. Nobody else is going to judge you fairly."

Peyton stood up from the table and stretched. She allowed Indigo to lead her back to the sofa, where she tucked her feet under her again, Indian style, and rested her head along the top edge of the seat.

"Now, to answer your question—Reuben and I are indeed in two different places spiritually, and that was the one thing that gave me pause. But when he described your grandparents, and how he had been raised, I was reassured.

"Everything Reuben needs is right inside of him, waiting to burst forth," Peyton said. "The only thing holding God at bay in Reuben's life is Reuben, with his doubts and fears and anger over how your parents died. When it appeared that our relationship was growing serious and I knew I loved him, I started talking to God about whether this was right.

"God helped me see past Reuben's defenses and even his lingering pain, to the man who's tucked inside the tough 'little boy' exterior the world sees," Peyton continued. "He showed me that Reuben was a good man, and a man after his own heart. Reuben just needs to accept that about himself and stop running from himself and everyone else. I had a peace when I said 'yes' to his marriage proposal that in God's timing, he would come around and share my faith. In the meantime, I just have to be thankful for the loving, giving husband he is and share my light with him without badgering him. God's going to do the rest. I know he's working it out."

Indigo was humbled. She had never given much thought to how their biological parents' deaths could still be affecting him as an adult.

I've been hating on my brother when I should have been praying for his wounded soul.

Her disdain and avoidance had only heaped coals on the fire he had lit around himself. She was ashamed. "I don't know everything, do I?"

Peyton shook her head.

"This family likes to keep secrets, and I hate that," Indigo said, trying to quell her frustration. "But you see where it gets us? Misunderstandings. Broken relationships. Surprise disappearances. We've got to stop this, but how?"

"The solution is simple, but implementing it isn't," Peyton said. "We break negative patterns by giving everything to God. All of it. Our desires, our fears, our frustrations, our need for revenge. When we hand all of it over and go on about our business, he works it all out without us having to break into a sweat or lift a finger. I've seen it happen time and time again in my own life.

"And that's why I allowed myself to fall for your brother, because I knew that he was a man who would catch me if I ever physically faltered or needed emotional strength. And regardless of whether he acknowledged it, I knew that his strength came from God, because of how and when it was instilled in him.

"Reuben has let a mountain of hurt chink away at his self-confidence, at his faith, and at his being, but even so, he's been able to be such a giving person. Anybody who has that kind of capacity when they're wounded is going to be amazing when they're healthy, and I know that God is going to heal him. That's really why we moved back to Jubilant, Indigo. This is all part of God's plan to bring Reuben back to him, and from what I'm hearing tonight, to bring you closer to him too."

Indigo was seconds from baring her soul when the ringing cell phone saved her. She glanced at the number and saw 212 again. Knowing it was probably Sasha, she decided not to answer. It was Saturday evening, and she had company.

"Go ahead and take the call," Peyton said. "I'll get my deck of Braille playing cards so I can beat you at Bid Whist."

She felt her way to the edge of the sofa and rummaged through her purse while Indigo strode to the kitchen.

"Indigo Burns here."

"Thank God."

Indigo pulled the phone away from her ear and stared at the receiver, to make sure she was hearing correctly. This couldn't be Sasha Davies calling.

"Hello?"

"Indigo?"

"Yes?"

"Hi, it's Sasha. I didn't mean to catch you off guard, I'm just so glad that you answered."

What was the world coming to? Indigo was eager to hear this. She sat at the small round table in her kitchen and waited.

"I know where Yasmin is."

She must be losing it. She was hearing things. "What did you say?"

"Your sister Yasmin is here in New York. She has been living with me for a few weeks, but now she's gone."

Peyton appeared in the kitchen doorway, holding the deck of cards.

"Sasha, I need you to repeat yourself. Are you telling me that Yasmin has been in New York with you for nearly a month? Why are you just now calling? No—better yet, just tell me where she is!"

Sasha sighed. "That's the problem, Indigo. I don't know anymore. She got upset with me when I enforced her curfew and we had a fight. I came home three days ago from the office and she had packed her bags and left me a note, informing me that she didn't need me to make it. She has other friends in the business too.

"That's why I'm calling. Those so-called 'other friends' are bad news. Every reputable agent in New York knows they use girls up and spit them out. I'm worried."

Indigo's mouth fell open. She couldn't believe she had been a phone call away from her sister all this time. Yasmin had had the good sense to run somewhere safe, but now it sounded like she was getting sidetracked.

"Did she come straight to you when she got to New York, Sasha?" Indigo asked.

The lack of a reply was her answer.

"Why didn't you call then?"

"She's eighteen now," Sasha said. "She can make her own decisions and sign her own contracts."

Indigo understood. Her sister was being groomed for Ford Models again, but at a price and at a pace that Sasha preferred. Just like any good talent scout or agent would, she was going to take care of herself through Yasmin and whoever else she could.

"So your meal ticket's gone now and you're calling to tattle."

Indigo knew she had gone too far when Sasha didn't respond. She could feel the woman seething through the phone.

"I'm sorry, Sasha. I'm just worried about my sister. I appreciate the fact that you did call. What do you suggest my family and I do to find her, to get her back home?"

"I don't know that she'll be coming home anytime soon, Indigo. She has jobs lined up with some of the upper-echelon fashion houses through next spring. She'll be working pretty steadily, just like she wants."

"Who vetted her contract, Sasha?" Indigo reigned in her anger by speaking slowly. "Slave labor is against the law, you know."

"She's better off with me than where she's headed." Sasha didn't sound a bit remorseful. "I don't know how you could possibly track her down in New York if she doesn't want to be found, but if she touches base with you, let her know she's headed for trouble. Any big missteps could ruin her chances for a reputable career with Ford or any other A-list agency."

Indigo felt trapped and helpless. What could she do from Jubilant, Texas? "Do you have her new cell number, Sasha?"

Sasha hesitated, but passed it along. "She's not answering my calls. Maybe you'll get lucky."

Indigo thanked Sasha again and ended the call with a promise to tell Yasmin to contact her regarding her contract. She quickly dialed Yasmin's new number and held her breath, unsure of what to say first if her sister picked up.

But Yasmin didn't answer. The best thing Indigo could do was reiterate Sasha's warnings about the questionable modeling agencies, and beg her to at least call.

"Mama and Daddy need to hear your voice, and I do too. Don't give up your dream, but don't give up on us, either, Yasmin. Call us."

Indigo shut off the phone and sank into a chair, deflated. Peyton cautiously crossed the room until she felt the edge of the table and searched for the seat across from Indigo.

"The good news is that she's alive and well, and that she's been staying in a safe place," Peyton said.

Indigo nodded and remembered that Peyton couldn't see. "You're right. But how do I call Mama and Daddy and tell them what I just learned, especially that she's probably not coming home or finishing high school? They can't take much more."

Peyton rested her chin in her hand.

"Remember the conversation we just had, about not keeping secrets or hiding truths? Now might be a good time to stop holding back. The truth sets all of us free—from fear, from manipulation, from the need to be right. It is what it is. At the very least, you can let them know that she has been making safe choices thus far, and the hope is that she'll continue. Tell them that you've left her a message and urged her to call. Then we all can pray for the same thing: for Yasmin to be wise and mature and to make it home safely, despite all that glitters before her right now."

Indigo flipped open her cell phone and pressed the speed dial code for Mama and Daddy's home number. She passed the phone to Peyton.

"Here, sis. Help me out."

26

Max gave it to him straight.

"You think you're the man and you can heal yourself. Ain't gonna happen, Reuben. You can't cure whatever you're wrestling with without some professional help, and there's nothing wrong with that."

Reuben wasn't sure how he and Max had landed on the subject of his nightmares, but somehow it had all come out during the pickup game of basketball they launched into after Reuben lost his third game of pool.

The recurring dreams, the decision to move back to Jubilant to fix his mistakes, the frustration over his unsuccessful attempts—until just recently—to reconcile with Indigo, the guilt over Yasmin running away.

Max seemed unfazed, and he had a ready answer: Reuben was trying to do the impossible. "It's like opting to perform surgery on yourself, and without anesthesia."

Reuben attempted to mask his embarrassment with lightheartedness. "I thought colored folk, especially men, had issues with going to counseling. You seem just the opposite."

Max paused and tossed the ball to him. "We do have hang-ups about it, but that's why we stay stuck in our mess," he said. "My mother took my sister and me to counseling when she decided to leave my father. I was fifteen and angry and rebellious. I didn't want to go and acted a fool for the first few sessions. But when I let my guard down and started to get real, those sessions helped me figure out how to handle my pain and disappointment over my parents' divorce."

Reuben paused with the ball positioned for a shot. "You got all of that in counseling. How long did you go?"

"For about a year." Max stole the ball from Reuben's grip. "It was the worst and the best year of my life."

"How could it be both?"

"Because out of the devastation of losing my intact family, I discovered how to find lessons in life's difficulties. The therapist helped me determine what steps I needed to take to become the man I wanted to be. He showed me how to make choices that would matter for a lifetime, not just for short-term gains or pleasure."

Reuben chuckled. "I'm almost thirty-two. If I don't know who I am by now, I'm in trouble."

Max ran alongside him and nudged him with his elbow. "You're moving too slow to be the same age as me. Step it up!"

They played for a few more minutes, until Max tossed what he called the final throw and conceded his loss to Reuben.

"Good game, man."

A short time later, on the way to his car, Reuben brought up the subject again. "I enjoyed myself tonight man, and thanks for listening. It's not often that I open up like that."

Max grabbed Reuben's shoulder and looked him in the eye. "It's all good, Reuben. We're family. I could tell something was on you the night we went to Bible study. I'm here if you need to talk, but Pastor Taylor is a good resource too. Not many people know it, but he's a professional psychologist as well as a theologian."

Reuben's eyes widened. "But he worked at a homeless shelter, he said."

Max nodded. "Yes—as the assistant director, a role he was able to assume because of his undergrad and master's degrees in psychology."

The revelations just kept coming. This was good information, though. If Pastor Taylor could confidentially advise him, he wouldn't have to drive so far for help. He must be trustworthy if Max recommended him.

The men hugged and slapped palms, and Reuben slid behind the steering wheel of his SUV. He lowered his driver's side window, so he could continue his conversation with Max.

"How's Indigo feeling about me these days?" He had promised himself he wouldn't put Max on the spot, but he couldn't help it.

Max shrugged. "Ask her, Reuben. Go straight to the source. The more you do that, the more you'll find those nightmares losing their power."

Under normal circumstances he would have stayed as far away as possible from anyone who showed as much disdain as Indigo had. But he knew a lot of it was his fault. He had summoned the courage to tell two people the truth—Peyton knew everything and Max knew enough to be helpful. He was getting close to home base, but he hadn't hit a homerun yet.

He wondered, for the first time since coming home, what it would be like to sit Indigo down, and his parents, and simply tell it all. The thought both terrified and intrigued him. Max was right, though—something had to give; he couldn't continue down this path.

He looked up the church address and phone number on his navigation system, and although it was Saturday night, he left a message on Pastor Taylor's private voice mail, requesting an appointment.

Reuben ended the call and sighed. Already he felt lighter. He was going to work through this, and God help him, he just might be alright.

27

Reuben parked on the street in front of Mama and Daddy's house because the driveway was already full. He was stopping by to pick up Charles David before swinging by Indigo's place to get Peyton. To his surprise, Aunt Melba, Rachelle and Gabe, and even Indigo were there. Why hadn't Peyton called to let him know where she was?

Yasmin.

If she had come home and he were the last to know, he might hit the roof. He jogged up the path to the house and pushed on the door to see if it was open. It was.

He strode to the family room and found everyone gathered around the desktop computer positioned against the far wall.

"What's going on? Max and I weren't invited to the party?" he asked and approached the group to see what had captured their attention.

They were scrolling through a list titled "B List Modeling Agencies" and jotting down the names of places with particular zip codes.

Peyton wiggled through the group to his side and hugged him. She wrinkled her nose, but didn't comment. Reuben knew his basketball sweat was unappealing.

"We tried to call you and Max, but no one answered at the house or on either of your cells," she said. "I got here and got engrossed and didn't think to call back and leave a message. Sorry, babe."

He remembered the basketball game. They had been outside and probably hadn't heard the rings. Max would probably show up shortly, if they'd left him a voice mail.

"What's going on? Have we figured out where Yasmin might be?"

Peyton filled him in on Indigo's chat with Sasha Davies. "We came over to tell your parents and they called Melba and Rachelle and Gabe and decided to try and figure out where she might be headed."

Reuben shook his head. He wanted his sister home safe and sound too, but unless they had more information, this seemed like a wild-goose chase. "Indigo, would any of your friends from your grad school days know about the places models hang out, or the names of modeling agencies notorious for scamming young girls? That might help narrow the focus."

He saw a glimmer of respect in her eyes, and his heart skipped a beat.

"Great idea, Reuben," she said, without a trace of her usual animosity. "I'll get my PDA and see whose numbers I still have."

She trotted off to find her purse, and Reuben searched the room for Charles David, who wasn't scampering around as usual.

"Where's my little man?" he asked.

"He was bathed and in jammies by the time Indigo and I got here," Peyton said. "He and his Grammy had decided he could spend the night, they just hadn't broken the news to us yet."

Mama and Daddy sat on the edge of their seats, watching as Rachelle and Gabe scrolled through the agencies, looking for clues. Fifteen minutes later, they printed the long list and logged off the computer.

"This could be impossible, with this many modeling agencies," Gabe told Mama and Daddy. "This really doesn't help us at all."

Melba pushed her chair away from the computer and stood up. "Let's give this a rest," she said. "Come on, everybody, get in a circle."

Reuben wasn't sure where this was headed, but since no one else balked, neither did he. Indigo returned to the family room just in time to close the gap. She hesitated before joining the group.

Melba gave her a pointed look. "We're waiting on you, Miss Lady."

Indigo stepped into position, and for the first time in he didn't know how many years, Reuben and his sister clasped hands. He was to her left, and Rachelle was to her right.

Reuben knew she felt uncomfortable, but he was still grateful.

Aunt Melba cleared her throat and looked at her sister. "Irene, and Charles, we're all thankful for the call Indigo received tonight that let us know the baby girl in our family is okay. We all might want to choke her right now, but she's okay.

"We've spent the past hour looking online for clues about places in New York she might be searching for work or even housing, but we all know that it would take a miracle to pinpoint the right place, out of the thousands of possibilities in even a small section of that city.

"We're going to pray in a minute and ask God to protect Yasmin and give her wisdom, and for her to come home safe and sound. But I have to be real, here. We're going to have to let her go too."

Reuben's heart constricted when Mama's eyes widened in alarm. Daddy frowned.

Aunt Melba nodded. "I know. That seems at odds with the prayer. But it's really not. We can't ask God to watch over her and still give us the puppet strings. We've got to let her go and allow her to make her own choices and find her way to him. Because she could come home tomorrow with the wrong spirit or attitude. We want her in fellowship with him first, and then with us. That order is important."

In that moment, Reuben got it. The order of his priorities had been all wrong too. He'd been running from God, thinking he'd find the peace and healing he needed in the opposite direction. Aunt Melba had just clarified what Peyton had been subtly telling him all along—it was only through God that he'd find everything he needed to recover. Not in spite of the Creator, but because of him.

Reuben's thoughts turned to Pastor Taylor's recent Bible study revelation, about the death of his first wife. He'd had to go through that pain to find himself in a moment, twenty years later, where he could minister to others from a position of healing. He had been broken, but now he could be a blessing.

Reuben wanted to weep. He turned toward Indigo and peered into her eyes. She couldn't read him as well as his wife could, but he knew she had witnessed his shift.

He didn't know what all of this meant, but as he bowed his head and listened to Daddy start off what would be a collective prayer for Yasmin and each other, he felt at ease in this stance for the first time in what seemed like forever.

When his turn came, he didn't squirm and squeeze Peyton's hand to cue her to help him. This time, he spoke for himself, with a wobbly heart, and without flowery language.

"It's me, God, Reuben. I know you don't hear from me often, and really, I don't have any right to be standing here asking you to do anything for my sister, or for me. But God, if you'll forgive me and give me another chance . . . I want to try to do better. Please take care of my sister and help her turn to you for answers. Keep her safe, and let her know we love her and want to help her. Help us find Yasmin, or lead her home . . . Amen."

As the formal prayer moved on to Peyton, Reuben continued his dialogue with God in silence.

He asked the Lord to give the family the strength to accept Yasmin's choices and each other's. He also asked God to help him get well, and to find the courage to do whatever that might take.

28

Reuben didn't feel out of place in worship service this morning for the first time in years, even though he still didn't understand all of the rules and traditions Peyton seemed to know despite never having seen them.

How, for example, could she be familiar with the stereotypical black Baptist church "tip"—the practice of raising one's index finger and tiptoeing out of service to use the restroom or meet another urgent need while the minister was in mid-sermon? For a blind woman, she was on top of things.

Today, a week after his heart-to-heart talk with Max, and the family prayer gathering at Mama and Daddy's, he sat next to Mama with a renewed spirit. Everything held meaning for him: the Scripture the teenager read from Proverbs about trusting in God and leaning not on one's own understanding; the hymn "Amazing Grace," which was so fitting for his sudden about-face; the message Pastor Taylor had just delivered about accepting that even among Christians, there were jewels in the rough that needed to be buffed and polished, or in other words, nurtured and loved, so that their value and talents could be recognized and appreciated.

He waited until the crowd died down and then approached

Pastor Taylor after service to make the request he had rehearsed in his mind several times on the way to church this morning.

"I was wondering if you had time to meet with me privately for some . . . counseling? There are a few things I'd like to get your take on, if you don't mind."

Pastor Taylor shook his hand and nodded his head toward a side entrance and exit to the sanctuary, to the hall that led to his office. "No time is better than the present, son. Let me say hello to these few folks behind you and we'll head to my office.

"Marlayne," he called to his wife, "can you talk with Sister Peyton for a little bit and let the girls play with Charles David? I need to have Brother Reuben take a look at the computer in my office."

Reuben immediately relaxed. This wasn't going to appear to the congregation like he had asked for help; Pastor Taylor needed his advice. He was instantly embarrassed that appearances mattered, but he couldn't beat himself up. He worked for the mayor and operated under a certain level of scrutiny; being discreet was important.

When they reached the office, Pastor Taylor unlocked the door and ushered Reuben inside. He pointed to his computer and grinned. "Take a look—so I can't be called a liar in the Lord's house."

Reuben laughed and pointedly stared at Pastor Taylor's flat screen monitor. He sat across from the preacher's massive mahogany desk, filled with neatly organized stacks of paper, and exhaled. Now that he was here, where should he begin?

"At the beginning," Pastor Taylor suggested.

Reuben frowned. "Do we have that much time?"

"Give me the CliffsNotes version," Pastor Taylor said. "When did your dilemma start and what kind of feedback or help can I give you?"

"It started almost twenty years ago when my parents died in a car crash that I survived." Reuben felt odd describing the experience so matter of factly. "I was called the miracle child because I didn't die after being trapped in my seatbelt, inside the car, for nearly twelve hours.

"Everyone assumed I spent that time alone, calling for help. My grandparents don't even know that my mother, Meredith, lived for a while. We talked, and she made me promise to take care of my sisters. Indigo was seven and Yasmin was about eight months old at the time. I was twelve."

Pastor Taylor sat back in his seat and ran his hand over his slick head. "My goodness, son," he finally said. "Did I hear you say that you've never shared this conversation with anyone, not even Brother Charles and Sister Irene? May I ask why?"

Reuben shrugged. "I can't think of a rational reason. I was deeply hurt over my parents' deaths. To tell you the truth, I've been angry with God ever since then for ignoring my pleas and taking them from me. Mama and Daddy—um, that's what I call my grandparents—never asked me directly what happened or what I was doing while I waited to be rescued, and I never offered the information. Living with the memories of those hours was hard enough.

"The added responsibility of trying to handle my loss and take care of my sisters' needs too just seemed to be too much for me. So I kept that conversation and that promise to myself, thinking if no one knew about it, it would be okay if I wasn't able to keep it." Reuben took a deep breath, then sighed heavily.

"But it was the last thing I'd said I'd do for my biological mother, and even if no one else knew, I did. The older I got, the more it ate me up inside."

"You were twelve when you made that promise, son," Pastor

Taylor said gently. "What do you think your mother wanted you to do? How could a twelve-year-old take care of a seven-year-old and a baby? Do you think she meant for you to take her request so literally?"

Reuben looked away from Pastor Taylor's probing eyes and let that possibility ruminate in his spirit. Could it be that Mom hadn't been asking him to carry the weight of his sisters' well-being on his shoulders?

"She might have simply been asking you to stay close to them, to love them unconditionally," Pastor Taylor said. "If your mother was injured and fading in and out of consciousness, she might not have been able to tell you step by step what she meant, but she sounds like she was a great parent. I don't think she would have wanted you to stop living yourself in order to take care of Yasmin's and Indigo's physical and emotional needs—do you?"

Reuben shrugged. He hadn't known what to think all of these years. In his mind, the problem had mushroomed as they aged and life became more complicated at home. "Mama's drinking was in full swing just before I left, and Daddy coped by checking out. I felt like I was going to lose it if I didn't leave. I went off to college and really never came home again. But that triggered even more guilt, because I was leaving my sisters behind in this dysfunctional situation. Indigo knew it and caught the brunt of keeping up the façade by herself. I had copped out on my promise to my mother and didn't bother to check in enough to make sure Indigo was hanging in there. Before, we had at least leaned on each other. Now she was in it alone."

Reuben's eyes swelled with tears. "I still haven't shared with her what I've told you today, Pastor Taylor, I guess because I'm ashamed of myself for failing," he said. "But I have asked her to forgive me, and she's been working on it really hard."

Pastor Taylor put his palms together, as if in prayer, and leaned toward Reuben. "You know what will make her task easier?"

Reuben nodded. "Telling her all of this, and letting her decide for herself where to land."

Pastor Taylor sat back and smiled. "You already know what to do, Reuben. Did you even need me?"

Reuben nodded. "Yes, sir. I need your prayers, and maybe even your advice on how to share this information with my entire family. They deserve to know the full truth, and maybe when I share it, my nightmares will go away."

Pastor Taylor looked surprised. "You've been having nightmares? For how long?"

"Nightmares and occasional panic attacks. Ever since I became a father. Having Charles David kicked my guilt into overdrive. That's why I finally came home—to make amends to my sisters and to get him acquainted with this side of his family."

Pastor Taylor nodded. "Just know that you're on the right path. Talking about this and sharing these long-held secrets kill the 'night dragons,' as I call them. When you take the power away from having a secret, your dreams are your own again.

"You've also been struggling with survivor's guilt—the very thing I faced when I questioned why I should go on after Farrah was murdered.

"Stop feeling guilty that you made it through the crash all those years ago and trust that because you did, you owe it to God, and to your parents, to find out your strengths and use whatever gifts and talents you possess to glorify God, and to perhaps draw others to him too." Reuben absorbed the advice and held his tears in check.

"If we were Catholic, I'd tell you to consider yourself absolved and to go in peace," Pastor Taylor said. "Instead, just know that

Jesus paid the price a long, long time ago for any sin or guilt you might be harboring a long, long time ago. You keep sinning anew every time you pick up that issue again and try to manage it yourself. Just give it to God and let him use it to bring you, and others, closer to him. I've seen him do it time and time again.

"This won't be an easy or quick process, Reuben. If you want me to walk through this with you, I'm here. We can schedule some regular times to talk, outside of church and Bible study."

Reuben nodded. "Max told me you're a psychologist. I think I would like that." He hesitated, not wanting to offend Pastor Taylor, but needing to be honest.

"What is it, son?"

"I know how gossip can spread through a church like wildfire. I really don't want my business in the streets. I'd like to keep this confidential. If that's not possible because you have a staff that schedules your appointments, or because your secretary types your meeting notes or whatever, I'll have to make other arrangements."

Reuben sat back in his chair and clenched his fists as he waited for Pastor Taylor's reply. He couldn't believe he had spoken so boldly to a man of God, but he knew he'd never feel comfortable sharing the issues he struggled with if he had to worry about those details somehow getting leaked.

Pastor Taylor seemed unfazed. "I got you," he said. "Tell you what: let's plan on meeting once a week at my home office. I live in south Jubilant, not far from downtown where you'll be working. We can meet for morning coffee, for lunch, or on any evening except Mondays or Wednesdays, when I have church business to attend to. That way, it's off-site and we can just be two dudes hanging out.

"Believe it or not, I've got skills on the court too. We can shoot a few hoops while we talk if you'd like."

Reuben grinned. God had answered his prayer. "Deal, Pastor. Let me know when we can start. I'm ready to get past this, so I can be there for my family like they need me to be."

Both men stood, and Pastor Taylor walked around the desk to shake his hand.

"God's getting ready to birth something in you, Reuben. You just get ready."

29

Indigo's School of Visual Arts classmate had done some research and it wasn't pretty.

"I checked around and here's what I was told," said Victoria Nape, a fashion photographer living in Greenwich Village with her TV-producer husband. "Accolade Models and Sensational Talent are two of the agencies that seem reputable but lure girls into posing nude and signing contracts that strip them of their rights to the images or to very much money. I hope your little sis hasn't landed in either of those.

"I remember her cute little self. I'm not surprised that she's still modeling—she had the build for it and the face. I'll keep my eyes and ears open and let you know if I see or hear anything, okay?"

Indigo ended the call feeling more discouraged than ever, but she tried to mask her concern for Mama's benefit.

"What did she say?"

Mama sat across the table from her, sipping her second cup of morning coffee and fidgeting. Now that they'd had some word from Yasmin, even secondhand, she was more anxious than ever to get the girl home.

Indigo kept running through her mind Sasha's warning that

Yasmin had no intentions of coming home, especially when she was landing modeling gigs. She didn't share that information with Mama, though; neither she nor Daddy could handle that right now.

Daddy strolled in with the newspaper and laid it in front of Mama. "Guess who made the front page today?"

Mama's eyes grew wide. "I knew I should have declined the honor. How am I going to accept this award and my child has run away? Makes no sense."

Indigo put her hand over top Mama's. "You've got to stop thinking that way, Mama. Yasmin's decision to leave home was about her, for her. You can't keep placing the burden of her choices on your shoulders. You've spent the past decade telling kids and teens throughout Jubilant how you overcame alcohol abuse and how the effects of your drinking impacted each of us.

"It still does. We all know how Reuben handled it, and Yasmin too—she became bulimic. I guess I played the martyr. My anger at Reuben was my crutch. It has taken all these years, and the honest assessment of a few good friends like Max and Shelby, to realize that by holding on to my teenage resentment, a big part of me was stuck in adolescence. In order for me to grow up and get ready to be a good wife, I've had to shed some of that stuff."

Mama smiled and shook her head. "Speaking of you being a wife, how is the planning process going? I've been totally out of the loop with your wedding details, haven't I? I'm sorry. I've just been so busy helping Reuben, Peyton, and Charles David get settled. I know you—you've got everything under control, right?"

Indigo debated whether to tell Mama that she had firsthand knowledge of how well Peyton and Reuben had their lives under control. They were all settled into Jubilant and into their neighborhood and didn't need Mama's oversight. She, on the other hand, needed as much help as she could get to prepare for her wedding day and beyond. Based on Mama's flippant comment, however, it didn't seem as if she were offering.

Normally this would have fueled Indigo's anger. Today, Mama's nonchalance simply saddened her.

30

Indigo had a list of wedding expenses in front of her when Shelby called. She sat at the small table in her kitchen with a calculator and notepad.

If little else got done this morning, she was going to make a final decision about November 15. Either she was walking down the aisle at St. Peter's Baptist Church or she and Max were boarding a plane to Jamaica with their best friends in tow to witness their vows.

The latter option was sounding more appealing, especially as they debated whether to use the money they would have spent on the wedding to make a larger down payment on the house they wanted. So far, the house they'd fallen in love with was still available, but that could change at any time, if a buyer walked in and made an offer.

"Why do you sound so preoccupied this early on a Saturday morning?" Shelby asked. "Surely you can't be processing photos."

Indigo paused and peered at her list. *Wedding gown*—$2,800 on sale. Paid in full. *Bridesmaid dresses*—$200 deposit to have the dresses shipped to her for tailoring. Balance of $900 due from bridesmaids upon dresses' arrival. *Flowers*—$1,000 for floral arrangements for bride and bridesmaids, fresh flowers for the sanctuary and at the reception hall. $250 deposit paid. *Cake*—$500. Ordered. To be paid for on wedding day. *Photographer*—$500 paid with sitting for wedding portrait. $1,000 due after wedding day photo shoot. *Reception hall & catering*—$500 nonrefundable deposit paid. $3,500 due on November 1.

Indigo could add a few more things to the list, but these were the biggest ticket items, and among the most critical.

She read the list to Shelby.

"I could keep my wedding gown for Jamaica, and we could have a small backyard reception on November 15, to celebrate our nuptials. We could have the cake then. You know it will still be warm enough here in Texas, and we won't have to worry about the summer humidity. That way, everything won't go to waste."

"Sounds interesting," Shelby said. "But I don't understand—why are you shifting plans this close to your big day? You've been dreaming about this wedding for a long time. Are you sure you want to give that up? If so, why? Isn't your mom coming around?"

Indigo sighed. "Yes and no, Shel. She's better, but she still hasn't zeroed in on this wedding. To tell you the truth, I think she's half wishing I'd put it on hold, to let everything else that's going on settle down. That's not something I'm willing to do, though. Max and I are ready to get married. We might change the logistics and the location, but I've promised him that I'll become his wife in November, and that's a done deal.

"My big question now is, can you and Hunt join us in Jamaica? Max's sister and her husband say they will, and so will Reuben and Peyton, Max's two good friends from college, and Nizhoni. They would be the other members of our wedding party.

"Nizhoni is such a great friend—she's working on getting us reduced airfare with her airline employee discount. Finally makes me glad that she left us here in Jubilant to fly the friendly skies."

Shelby's silence unnerved Indigo. Was her best friend going to let her down and refuse to come?

"You know I'll be there if I can, Indie," Shelby began, but Indigo cut her off.

"If you can? What's that supposed to mean?"

"If you'd let me finish talking, Miss Thang, I'll tell you."

Indigo had to laugh at herself. "Sorry for being rude. I guess since I've taken the pressure off Mama and Daddy, I've transferred it to you. You were trying to tell me something?"

"That's more like it!" Shelby said.

Indigo knew her friend was getting a kick out of setting her straight.

"As I was trying to say," she said and chuckled, "if I can get permission to travel internationally, and it's safe, Hunt and I'll be there to share your special day. You know we love you guys. You're my other sister."

Indigo laid her pen down and settled back in her chair. She crossed her arms and frowned. "Permission? Talk to me, Shel. You and Hunt okay? Everything at work going okay?"

Shelby chuckled. "Let me stop stringing you along. Girl, I am eight weeks pregnant. I need—"

Indigo's shrieking drowned out Shelby's words. She settled down to catch her breath and wondered if Shelby could feel her beaming through the phone. "Sorry, Shel. I didn't hear anything you just said. I can't believe I'm going to be an auntie!"

"I was saying, I need to ask my doctor if it's okay for me to fly to Jamaica. I don't want to miss your wedding, if I can help it."

"You do what you need to do to keep you and the baby healthy. You know I'll understand. I'm so excited!"

Indigo paused. "You are too, aren't you? This is good news, right?" Indigo recalled Shelby's ambivalence when they discussed this topic during their recent weekend in Dallas.

Shelby chuckled. "Yes, Indie. It's all good. I'm very happy. Terrified, but happy all the same."

"How are you feeling? How's Hunt?"

"The morning sickness is finally going away, as I get closer to twelve weeks," Shelby said. "Mine and Hunt's. He's been experiencing some of the signs of a sympathetic pregnancy."

"You're kidding," Indigo said. Then she zeroed in on what she really wanted to know. "I mean, how are you feeling emotionally? Are you ready for this?"

"Oh." Shelby said. "That. You know, Indigo, I just turned it over to God and asked him to lead me. I love my husband and Hunt loves me. I know that without a doubt. We've talked about my insecurities and his. We're on solid ground. This baby is a gift. You and Max are going to make great godparents."

Indigo wanted to cry. "I can't wait, Shel. You just get to the islands for my wedding. We'll have some amazing tales to share with our little bundle of joy. Or bundles. Twins would be nice."

Shelby responded with a dial tone. Indigo gripped the phone in surprise. Shelby had hung up on her? She laughed.

Indigo would call her back shortly, to remind her to check on her passport status. She couldn't get married without her best friend. If Shelby couldn't travel internationally, maybe they could find somewhere beautiful in the States to seal their union.

With all she and her family had been through in recent months, Indigo was less concerned about the pomp and circumstance of a wedding and more focused on building a solid marriage. Max was already walking through some tough issues with her and her family. This was the stuff husbands were made of, not the great tux and wedding dance they had been practicing.

Besides, both of them were practical. If Max sold his rancher, they combined their personal contributions to their wedding that her parents weren't covering, and added any additional savings outside of their emergency cushion, they would have a sizeable down payment for the house they both loved.

Max wanted to make as large a deposit as possible, to keep the mortgage payments in the range they had originally estimated would be manageable with their current careers and expenses. Scaling down the wedding would be worth it, long term.

And, Indigo had accepted that it would be stressful trying to pull off a festive event with Yasmin absent.

Shelby's announcement this morning had merely added a twist. Indigo picked up the phone to dial Max's number and share the news, but a text from Shelby came through before she could begin dialing.

> U sound like you're in such a good space. So glad. & Reuben's part of the picture 2? God does work miracles. Whatever you decide, your wedding day is going 2 B blessed. Luv u, Shel.

Indigo's heart warmed. She accepted the blessing right here and now and sent up an arrow prayer on Shelby's behalf. Her friend had made all sound well this morning. She asked God to make it so—her marriage, her career decisions, her baby's health.

> Right back at ya, Shel. Luv u much.

Both of them were on the verge of something new and beautiful and she couldn't wait.

31

Getting here hadn't been easy, and Reuben had to admit that his pride had caused unwarranted delays.

Today was his fourth session with Pastor Taylor, and already, he felt like he could be himself and not worry about being ridiculed or gossiped about when he left. Already, he felt better about who he was and where he fit into his family.

It was long past time for him to lose the guilt over surviving the car accident.

"Did you have time to read any of the material I recommended about post-traumatic stress disorder?" Pastor Taylor asked this afternoon.

It was Thursday around lunchtime, and the midday sun streamed in through the solitary window behind him, just over his left shoulder. They were sitting in Pastor Taylor's home office, an expansive room built onto the rear of the house, with its own entrance and exit.

Reuben nodded. "I did, and I was floored. I can't believe that nearly twenty years after my parents' deaths, I could still be affected so deeply. I can't believe that after all this time, the accident contributed to my panic attacks."

Pastor Taylor leaned forward and rested his elbows on his desk.

He made a teepee with his fingers. “Your panic attacks *and* your nightmares. Why not, Reuben? When we stuff pain inside of us, instead of dealing with it head-on, it can’t stay bottled forever. Pressure pops the cork.

“Happens to veterans of war all the time. There are men and women walking the streets of this nation, who went to the first Gulf War in the early nineties, who are still suffering from all that they witnessed and experienced. The same is true for soldiers who came home last year from Iraq or Afghanistan.

“You experienced a devastating loss at a pivotal age,” he said. “Not only did both of your parents die, you witnessed their deaths, and then you had to grapple with the fact that you survived. That’s a lot for an adult to handle, let alone a child. Simply because of the fact that you never got help then, you never talked to anyone, it makes perfect sense that the trauma would haunt you.

“Add to that the fact that you never grieved, and you harbored this promise you made to your mother that you feel you didn’t keep.” Pastor Taylor shook his head. “I’m amazed that the panic attacks didn’t come sooner.”

Reuben chuckled. “Seems like I was able to keep it all together until I fell in love and became a father.”

Pastor Taylor nodded. “Exactly. You’d been able to suppress sincere, authentic emotions until then. When you married Peyton and when Charles David was born, these overwhelming feelings of love and protectiveness began competing for the space that the guilt and fear held.

“You aren’t superman, Reuben, and no one is requiring you to be. You need to give yourself permission to grieve the very deep loss you suffered, and to accept that part of the reason you ran away and stayed away was to emotionally protect yourself.”

Reuben squirmed in his seat. All this talk of healing and

surviving was a bit much. He felt safe talking to Pastor Taylor about it, knowing what he'd been through with his first wife, Farrah, but still, he felt naked.

Pastor Taylor sat back in his chair and folded his arms across his chest. "I see the wheels turning in your head. What are you thinking?"

Reuben shrugged. "I don't know. Just feeling . . . exposed, I guess. And wondering what's next."

Pastor Taylor chuckled. "Not used to sharing this much of yourself with someone else, right? I've been there."

"Peyton knows most of this, but that's different," Reuben said.

"Yes, it is," Pastor Taylor said. "She knows the vulnerabilities you've allowed to trickle out over your six years together, not the formal diagnosis for why you've been struggling. And it could be that you don't know all that's on her mind, because she's holding back to protect you."

Reuben frowned. Peyton wasn't one to shy away from the truth. She was usually straightforward about her concerns and her desires. But he remembered how upset she had been the night he had returned home from his spur-of-the-moment drive. He told Pastor Taylor about it, and explained that during his panic attack, somehow he had tried to grab his cell phone but had instead dropped it on the floor of the kitchen. Peyton had found it later the next morning when she swept the floor.

"What was different about her that night?" Pastor Taylor asked.

Reuben paused and looked past Pastor Taylor, out of the window. "I don't know how to describe it. I guess for the first time since I've known her, I saw fear in her eyes. I saw her in a weak moment. Being blind and in unfamiliar surroundings or situations never shake her confidence, but that night, she was frightened and helpless."

Reuben looked into Pastor Taylor's eyes. "It scared me, you know?"

"Why?"

"I think because for the first time, I realized that despite the fact that she's so independent and self-confident, she needs me," Reuben said. "She needs me to protect her, to love her, and to be healthy and whole for her."

"How does that make you feel?"

"Great, that on one hand, my wife is counting on me to meet these needs, but guilty on the other, because I know that unless I deal with the stuff that's been tormenting me, I'm a burden to her instead of a hero."

Pastor Taylor picked up his Bible and thumbed through it, until he found what he was looking for. "It's interesting that you used the word 'hero,' Reuben. Do you really think Peyton wants you to be her 'hero,' or does she simply want a healthy helpmate? We men like to add that extra level of machismo, but I'm almost certain that your wife isn't looking for you to scale mountains on her behalf; she just wants you to climb them with her. You can relax a little."

Reuben sat back in his chair and grinned. "Yes sir."

Pastor Taylor extended the Bible toward him and pointed to a passage that was already highlighted—Ephesians 2:8–9: *For it is by grace you have been saved, through faith—and this not from yourselves, it is the gift of God—not by works, so that no one can boast.*

Reuben read the passage, then looked at Pastor Taylor for help to decipher it.

Pastor Taylor closed the Bible and smiled. "Repeat it after me, Reuben: 'For it is by grace that I have been saved, through faith—not because of anything I've done; it is the gift of God—not my works, so I really can't boast.'"

Reuben repeated the passage as Pastor Taylor recited it, and for the first time, felt the words sink into his spirit. He had been baptized as a child, and in recent weeks, he had been attending the Wednesday night Bible study, but today, this particular Scripture resonated deeply enough to penetrate his core.

"You get it, son? I paraphrased the New International Version here, because I want you to understand it. You can't do any of this by yourself; you weren't designed for that. Your job is to love God, to trust God, and to build a solid relationship with him so that he guides your path and gets glory from every aspect of your life. You don't have to earn his love and his mercy, he gives it to you simply because you're his child."

The power of that revelation was overwhelming. It released Reuben—finally—from all that he'd been holding inside or fleeing from or trying to fix. In two Bible verses that he'd never read before, he found the freedom to be okay.

He opened his mouth to share what he was experiencing, but found that he couldn't speak. The lump that had formed in his throat was too big. Instead of words, tears erupted, and he couldn't stop them.

Reuben lowered his head and wept. He cried for Mom Meredith and Dad David, and for the little boy he used to be before the accident and their deaths traumatized him. He cried over the decisions he had made from his impaired state since then—going away to college and never coming back, getting married without inviting his family, uprooting Peyton from her native Seattle in the effort to heal himself.

As each scene from his life flashed before his eyes, he sobbed harder.

Pastor Taylor rose from his seat and pushed a box of tissue to the edge of his desk so that Reuben could reach it when he was ready. He came around the desk and patted Reuben's shoulder on his way toward the door.

"Let it all out, young man," he said. "You've kept those tears inside for too long. God is counting them for you and putting them in a bottle. You let go and give it all to him. You're going to be alright."

Pastor Taylor left the study and closed the door behind him.

When he was all alone, Reuben fell to his knees and bowed his head. He stayed in that position until the tears subsided. Then he spoke to God with a respect and reverence for him that had been absent since his parents' death.

"God, forgive me for being angry with you all of these years, and for not understanding that you didn't cause my pain—you were there to walk through it with me." Reuben choked out the prayer just above a whisper, and his voice quivered.

"Forgive me for hurting the people who loved me most. Please heal me and help me make it up to them, especially Mama and Daddy and Indigo. And please help me help my sister Yasmin."

And then, he was quiet. He sat there on his knees and rested his head on the chair, and let God's love envelop him. Tonight he was going to sleep well. The nightmares had no more space to call their own.

32

Mama and Daddy might not be ready to hear the truth, but Reuben had decided it was time.

His sessions with Pastor Taylor were giving him clarity, and he needed to own his role in his family's unbalanced dynamics.

He and Peyton invited his parents to join them for dinner, and after feasting on the meal Peyton had prepared, the five of them, including Charles David, were relaxing in the family room, forced at the boy's insistence to watch cartoons on Nickelodeon.

Peyton won him over by offering a treat—the chance to watch his shows from his parents' bed. Charles David dashed into the master suite before she changed her mind.

That left the four adults to themselves, and Daddy didn't waste time in picking up the remote and turning to ESPN.

Reuben watched golfing highlights with him and toyed with how to broach the subject he intended to address tonight before Mama and Daddy left. He could have kissed Peyton when she opened the conversation right where they needed to start: on Indigo.

"What do you guys think about the latest wedding plans?" Peyton asked.

Daddy lowered the TV volume and turned his attention to Peyton. "What do you mean? Indigo and Max's wedding?"

Peyton nodded. "They've gone from planning a big church ceremony to considering getting hitched in Jamaica to maybe hosting a ceremony on the beach in Florida. That last option was put on the list of possibilities just a few days ago."

Mama was floored. Reuben was stunned by her surprise.

"Haven't you been talking to her at all, Mama?" he asked.

Her stuttering and sputtering were answer enough.

"Mama," Peyton said. A mountain of disappointment dripped from that single word.

"Indigo needs you too, you know," Reuben said. He walked over to the sofa and sat next to his mother, who was flanked by Daddy on her left. "She needs both of you."

"What's that supposed to mean?" Daddy asked.

Reuben looked toward Peyton for help. She couldn't read his eyes, but he knew she'd understand his lack of response as an invitation to chime in.

She, too, moved closer to the sofa, opting to sit on the edge of the coffee table in front of her mother- and father-in-law.

"There's been a lot going on in this family in the past few months, and a lot of it stems from our move here from Seattle," Peyton said.

"That's been wonderful! What are you talking about?" Mama said.

Peyton nodded. "We agree. I have so enjoyed getting to know you better, and Charles David is just crazy about both of you. If he could split his time equally between our home and your place, he'd be in little-boy heaven."

Reuben picked up the conversation. "The reality is that my

absence and reappearance in the family over the past four years shook things up."

Mama and Daddy opened their mouths to protest. Reuben saw the alarm in Daddy's eyes. He raised his palm to quiet it.

"Don't worry—this conversation isn't setting you up for an announcement. We aren't leaving town or taking Charles David away. But there are some things I should have shared with you a long time ago that I've been struggling with since the car accident. And, on a different note altogether, there are some things Peyton and I have experienced and observed that we think haven't been fair to Indigo, or Yasmin."

"Not fair? What does that mean?" Daddy leaned forward to peer around Mama at Reuben, and frowned.

Reuben took a deep breath. "I know you guys love me and have been thrilled to have me home, but it's been somewhat overwhelming—your attention, that is. It's been nice for me, but I know that Indigo and Yasmin have suffered in silence for a long time."

"Suffered?" Now Mama was frowning.

Peyton patted Mama's knee. "They've felt neglected, and sometimes overlooked, and sometimes simply shoved aside so you could give our family your full attention. Believe me, we've appreciated it—we've basked in it. But they need you too."

"Are they jealous of my relationship with Reuben?" Mama asked.

Reuben and Peyton both shrugged.

"Could be, Mama," Peyton answered. "But you've given fuel to the fire. When was the last time you took Indigo to lunch or asked about her job? The fact that you didn't know the wedding plans were up in the air says a lot. She's been hurting for a long time and hasn't known how to address it with you. Reuben and I have been meeting with Pastor Taylor recently to help Reuben work through some things, and in that process, we've begun to shed a lot of façades. We've learned a lot about ourselves, and about the importance of speaking the truth in love on behalf of others too."

"For example?" Daddy asked. There was a thread of an attitude lurking beneath the question.

"For example, I never told you that Mom Meredith and I talked after the crash, that she told me goodbye before she closed her eyes and died after the car crash," Reuben said.

"What?!" Mama gasped. Her mouth fell open while Reuben filled her and Daddy in on that day's experiences. He told them about his guilt over the promise he made and never kept, and why he had fled to college and never returned.

"I find it interesting that we've visited so many times and even moved back, and not once did you ask why," Peyton said. "Not once did you ask Reuben what had kept him away for so long. Your dancing around the shadows allowed him to keep hiding behind them and made you work harder to keep the relationship comfortable." Peyton hesitated, and Reuben knew she was trying to choose her words carefully.

"That meant something else had to suffer, and it seems to us it was your connection to Indigo. We decided to have this conversation because even though she's putting on a mature front and trying not to complain, it has been hard for her to plan a life with Max when so many things with you all are unresolved. She needs you guys, just as much as we do."

"And don't worry," Reuben said. "We aren't going anywhere. You don't have to cling to us because you're afraid of that."

Peyton nodded. "That's the thing about fear—it makes us hold tighter to the things and people we love, and in doing so, we can sometimes squeeze the life right out of them. We want our family to be stronger than that and to be better than that, Mama."

Mama and Daddy exchanged glances and gripped each other's hands. Reuben saw in their expressions that Peyton had accurately diagnosed the problem.

"I guess I could live without being the consistent focus of your time and attention," Reuben joked, trying to put them at ease. "I can get used to sharing your time. Charles David might be another matter, but he'll be fine."

Reuben smiled and hugged Mama. She reciprocated.

"I am so sorry, son. You and Peyton got it all right. Daddy and I have had lots of questions, but we were afraid to run you off with them. Seems like while you stayed, though, everyone else took off. We couldn't see that choosing to dote on you was a choice to leave your sisters out in the cold.

"Between your return and Yasmin's disappearance, poor Indigo hasn't gotten much of me. How could she plan a wedding when I haven't been available to help her?"

"We love all three of you, you know?" Daddy said, and gazed at his hands.

Reuben extended his cell phone in his parents' direction. "I know, Dad," he said. "Tell Indigo that yourselves."

Mama held out a hand to take the cell phone. With the other, she stroked Reuben's face. "You've been through a lot, son," she said softly. "I'm sorry I haven't been a better listener and caregiver. If nothing else, I want you to know that I loved your mother, Meredith, as if she were my biological daughter, and I know how deeply she loved you and your sisters. If she made you promise to take care of Indigo and Yasmin, she meant to love them, nothing more. Meredith wouldn't have placed adult responsibilities on her little boy's shoulders, and even at age twelve, that's what you were to her—her little boy. Her promise was meant to keep the three of you close, not to burden you.

Had I known you were wrestling with this all of these years, I would have told you that a long time ago."

Reuben turned and hugged Mama tightly. He closed his eyes and accepted her embrace. "Thank you for that, Mama," he said. "I needed to know that."

Mama wiped her eyes and held up his phone. "How do I operate this fancy thing? Will you call Indigo for me?"

Reuben took the phone from her and punched Indigo's speed dial code. He peered at the clock on the wall.

At half past seven, Indigo was still on assignment, photographing an event at the Jubilant arts complex. But Mama and Daddy could leave her a message. It would make her day.

33

Indigo was as excited tonight as if she were the belle of the ball.

The fundraising gala was hosted by the mayor's wife, and so far the evening had been memorable and productive. For the first time since Reuben's move home, Indigo had been proud to share that he was her brother. Vivienne Henning and her husband lit up when she told them about the connection.

"He is doing wonderful work down at City Hall," Mayor Henning said, "and his wife and son are amazing."

Indigo nodded her agreement. "They are a great family."

She had been standing in the rear of the room, posing guests for society page photos for Jubilant's monthly magazine, when her cell phone rang. Reuben's number flashed on the screen.

Because she was working, she almost didn't answer. She realized, though, that he knew where she was. If he were calling, maybe there was an emergency.

She excused herself and stepped into the hallway to take the call.

Her eyes widened when she heard Mama's voice.

"Hey, baby, Daddy and I know you are working, but we wanted to give you a quick call and tell you that we love you," Mama said.

"Okaaay . . ." Indigo frowned. What had prompted this, and why a call now, in the middle of an assignment?

Daddy was in her ear next. "Indie, it's me. Look . . . Your mama and I have realized some things today . . . I just want to tell you that I love you and I'm sorry if you've felt neglected or cast aside. That was never our intention. Can you come over tomorrow afternoon so we can talk? We want to spend some time with you—you and Max, if you want."

"Sure . . . Daddy."

Indigo was at a loss for words. Had Reuben said something? Or Max? If she hadn't been working, she would have asked more questions. This would have to do for now, though. She needed to get back to shooting photos.

"Um, is everything okay, Daddy?"

She heard a wistfulness in his voice as he reassured her. "Yeah, baby. Your mother and I . . . we're finally learning to listen."

Indigo returned to work and tried to focus, but the call had thrown her off kilter. Daddy rarely expressed his emotions, yet he had seemed near tears. What had prompted this?

Later that evening, on the short drive home, Indigo made two phone calls. The first was to Reuben, to find out what he had said to their parents.

"I just told them the truth, Indie—we all need their love and attention," he'd said in a thick, sleepy voice. "Peyton, Charles David, and I aren't going anywhere, so they can stop hovering."

She was speechless for a few minutes. "Wow. Thank you, Reuben. I can't believe they listened."

"We're all changing, Indigo, for the better, I think," he said.

She heard him take a breath that sounded like a yawn.

Indigo was grateful. She had more questions, but the clock on her dashboard told her it was a few minutes before midnight. "Go back to sleep, brother. Sorry I woke you."

This time Reuben paused. "That sounds so good, Indigo."

"What?"

"To hear you call me brother."

She ended that call with tears in her eyes and looked up another number in her phone. Brian Harper's.

Today was her former fiancé's birthday, and before the clock reached midnight in Colorado, she wanted to wish him well.

Brian picked up on the second ring. "Hey, Ms. Burns," he said in his silky tenor voice. "I was beginning to think you had decided to break tradition."

Indigo smiled and turned into the entranceway of her townhouse community. "Just because I'm engaged now doesn't mean I can't call and wish you a happy birthday, like always."

"Will Max let you keep that up once you become Mrs. Shepherd?"

Indigo smirked. "Would you have let me keep it up if I had become Mrs. Harper?"

They both laughed.

"You've still got those comebacks ready, I see," Brian said. "I'm not going to touch that one. How are you, beautiful?"

"I'm doing great, Brian—wonderful, in fact," she said, thinking about the call from her parents earlier that evening. "How are you?"

"Life is good. I'm happy to be celebrating another birthday and happy to be living my dreams."

She was tempted to ask if that included a relationship with someone special, but shied away from the question, as usual. If Brian wanted to venture down that path with her at some point, she knew he would without her prying. The last time they had discussed his concerns about his sexuality, about three years ago, he had declared his intention to live a life of celibacy while pursuing the career he loved, so he could honor God without distraction.

Indigo was just thankful that he hadn't felt the need to go into seclusion or enter a monastery because they hadn't worked out as a couple.

"Still on course to become my favorite astronaut?" she asked.

Brian chuckled. "I am, my dear, I am. I submitted an application last month for the astronaut program. As you know, most applicants don't get accepted the first time around, but at least it will put me on NASA's radar."

Indigo smiled. She was proud of him. "Call me when you get the good news."

"Even if it's not my birthday?"

"Even if it's not your birthday," Indigo said. "Some things don't require a particular day on the calendar to celebrate."

They chatted for a few more minutes and promised to talk again soon, when Indigo's birthday rolled around, unless good news came from NASA before then.

"Tell Max I said hello, will you?" Brian asked.

Indigo stepped out of the car and grabbed her camera bag while juggling the cell phone with her other hand. "I will, Brian. He knows we trade birthday wishes. He'll be glad to hear that you're doing well."

"Tell him I said to keep taking good care of you, and I'll be doing even better. Good night, friend."

"Good night, Brian. Take care."

Indigo strode to her front door and set the camera bag down to find her key. She inserted it in the lock and stepped inside. Before she closed the door, she noticed the full moon filling the clear sky.

This was a night she would remember for a long, long time.

34

The last time a negative article had been published about the Burns family, Mama had been driving drunk and had caused an accident that left a young child injured. That was eleven years ago. This, Indigo decided, was much worse.

She had stopped by her parents' home this morning on her way to Max's studio and had found the two-page spread in a Dallas tabloid weekly newspaper splayed across the kitchen table. The section featured a smiling photo of Mama with the title "Jubilant's Woman of the Year?" on the left and an edited image of Yasmin, scantily dressed, striking a provocative pose with the subhead "Daughter Not So Squeaky Clean" on the right.

Indigo felt sick to her stomach as she perused the brief article that described how Yasmin had gone from a budding, reputable modeling career to getting lured into the seedy side of modeling, with one of the questionable agencies the family had seen on the list they printed from the computer a few weeks back. The featured picture was reportedly taken for a magazine that specialized in nude and semi-nude images.

The gaudy makeup she wore made Yasmin appear older than eighteen, and her eyes looked dark and empty, much like Indigo felt right now.

Indigo wondered which one of her parents had seen the article. Mama's car was gone, so she was probably out running her early morning errands.

Indigo laid the paper aside and slowly walked the hall to her parents' bedroom, where she tapped on the closed door. "Daddy, are you okay?"

He didn't respond, and she knew he was either praying or giving himself a hard time for his daughter/granddaughter's decisions. Indigo slid onto the floor and gathered her knees to her chest.

Oh Yasmin. Why?

She closed her eyes and opened her heart to God.

I don't know what to say, Lord. You know already what I'm feeling. You know already what all of us need. She's my sister and she's just eighteen. She's so young to have made such a mess of things. Help her, Lord, and help us.

Her cell phone rang, but she didn't have the heart to see who was calling, certain that they too had picked up a copy of the *Dallas Extra* at a local grocery store or other distributor. Before the call was routed to voice mail, though, she took a peek.

A blocked phone number registered on the caller ID. Indigo let the call go to voice mail; she had enough on her mind right now without trying to put on her professional demeanor and chit-chat with a potential client.

When the line was clear, she called Reuben.

He picked up after the first ring. "I know," he said. "One of my co-workers called about it and I ran out to find a copy this morning. Mama's coming in the door now. I don't think she knows yet. Let me call you back."

Mama breezed into Reuben's kitchen with a sunny smile and a bagful of yogurt she had picked up at the grocery store for Charles David.

"They were on sale, so I bought quite a few packages, since he goes through them so quickly," she told Peyton and made her way to the fridge. "I'm stopping by Indigo's next, to deliver some avocados and plums."

Peyton let her chatter incessantly before asking her to have a seat. When Reuben's friend had called an hour earlier, Reuben jumped in the car and returned with all of the copies of the *Dallas Extra* he found in a grocery store stand about five miles from home. By the time Mama stopped by, Reuben had already read the article and photo captions to Peyton.

How were they going to share this with Mama?

Peyton served Mama a cup of coffee and offered her a bagel.

"I'll take the coffee, but I'm watching my carbs," Mama said. "My doctor told me last week that I'm prediabetic."

Peyton poured herself a cup of brew, then sat across from her, in silence. Reuben was puttering around the sink, trying to quell his anxiety. Mama's heart was going to break.

Peyton reached for her hand, and he joined them at the table.

"Mama, there's something we need to show you, and it isn't pretty," Peyton said. "Reuben?"

Reuben picked up the newspaper and slid it before his mother's eyes. Mama seemed pleasantly surprised to see her picture, but as she looked and read further, her face fell.

Her eyes grew wide and she covered her mouth with her hand. "That's not my baby. That can't be my Yasmin. Oh my God."

She rose from the seat and headed for the door.

"Mama, where are you going?" Peyton called after her. She

turned her head toward Reuben. "I think she's too upset to drive. Can you stop her?"

Reuben ran out to the car, where Mama was fumbling to insert her key into the lock. The sight was strange, since her key ring included a button that automatically unlocked the door.

"I've made a mess of everything, haven't I? Some 'Woman of the Year.'" She spat out the words without looking at Reuben and focused on her mission.

Reuben gently took the keys from her and enveloped her in a hug.

They stayed that way a few moments before he spoke.

"Stop blaming yourself, Mama." He stepped back and looked into her sorrowful eyes. He put an arm around her thin shoulders and led her back inside the house. "We'll get through this. Somehow this is all going to work out for the best."

Reuben glanced up at the sky, wondering if the God he had only recently begun to trust would answer this time, and keep him from having just lied to Mama.

35

By the time Indigo remembered to check her voice mail messages, three hours had passed.

After discovering the newspaper at her parents' house and calling Reuben, she waited another half hour for Daddy to emerge from his bedroom. When he hadn't, she had been forced to go on to Max's studio to process a roll of film for a deadline assignment. Indigo was now on her way back to her parents' home. Mama had called and asked her to come over.

She pulled the cell phone from her purse and put it on speakerphone, to listen as she drove. She hit the voice mail key and nearly swerved off the road when she heard Yasmin's voice.

"Indie, it's me." She sounded so scared. And so young.

Indigo traveled through a traffic light and turned into a shopping center parking lot, where she put the car in park and listened.

"I don't know what to say . . . I think I messed up . . . call me?"

Yasmin left the phone number that had earlier flashed across Indigo's caller ID screen as a blocked number. Indigo wanted to kick herself. All these weeks she had been on pins and needles waiting to hear from her sister, and the one time Yasmin reached out, she let the call go to voice mail.

Indigo's hand shook as she dialed the number Yasmin had left.

Please, God, let her answer. Please. God.

Someone picked up on the third ring, but didn't say hello.

"Yas?"

Indigo heard her weeping.

"It's okay, Yasmin. Where are you? Are you safe?"

"Yes." The reply was a whimper.

She heard a voice in the background and it sounded as if Yasmin was passing the phone.

"Hello, Indigo?"

Sasha Davies voice filled the phone and Indigo gasped.

"What's going on? Sasha? Yasmin's back with you?"

"Yes, Indigo," Sasha said. "I started getting calls early this morning about questionable photos of her being published in some rag in Dallas, and I called her cell phone and asked her to get in touch with me immediately. We connected a couple hours ago. I don't know if you've seen the pictures—"

"We have," Indigo interrupted, worried about what all of this meant.

"Well, fortunately they aren't as risqué as I was led to believe," Sasha said, sounding relieved. "At least Yasmin is still partially clothed in them. Since there weren't any fully nude shots or X-rated poses, I think we can do some damage control and save her career."

Indigo wanted to believe, but part of her still didn't trust Sasha. "What does that mean? You aren't sending her home?"

This time Sasha paused. "Indigo, Yasmin is eighteen. She's an adult capable of making her own decisions. You can ask her, but I don't think she wants to come home. I'm trying to help her save her career. She already has some major gigs lined up, through my efforts. Even when I couldn't find her, I didn't cancel them, in hopes that she'd come to her senses and come back on board. Apparently, the scumbag who took those photos you saw in the tabloid lied to her and told her that I had hired him to do the session."

Indigo shook her head, struggling to believe that what she was hearing was real and not a soap opera update.

"Because we had argued, Yasmin was too proud to call me and verify everything he told her," Sasha said. "Now we've got to do damage control. Ford Models is issuing a press release indicating that Yasmin was scammed. We're also going to get her on the morning talk show circuit and use her experience to warn other aspiring models to avoid scam artists and criminals. So don't worry, some good is going to come out of this."

Indigo was perplexed. "You really do have my sister's best interest at heart, don't you?"

Sasha sighed. "Thank you, Lord. Finally she gets it."

Indigo's eyes widened.

"Indigo, I've had Yasmin's best interest at heart ever since I met her and your family almost five years ago. I don't wear my faith on my sleeve, but the God I represent wouldn't want me to do anything less.

"I know you and your parents want Yasmin to come home, but this is the decision she has made. If she weren't talented and excellent at what she does, I would be the first one trying to put her on a plane back to Texas. But she does have the look and the skill, and she can be really successful—if she doesn't make any more mistakes.

"Maybe your parents should try to compromise with her, instead of trying to force her to come home. This is where her heart is."

Indigo held the phone and nodded, although Sasha couldn't see her. Suddenly she remembered how crushed she had been the summer she lost her photography internship and wound up working as a receptionist in Aunt Melba's hair salon. She recalled her frustration and her fear that she'd never achieve her dreams, because her life seemed to be falling apart.

Those memories helped her decide. She was going to support Yasmin's choice, even if she didn't wholeheartedly understand it.

"Thank you, Sasha," Indigo said.

"For what?"

"For being who you are, and for being there for my sister. I will share your message, and Yasmin's wishes, with the rest of our family. Can I speak to her again?"

The logistics of Yasmin's permanent move to New York and completion of her high school degree would have to be worked out with Mama and Daddy, but Sasha had just put Indigo's mind at ease. The whole time the family had been fretting and praying, God had placed Yasmin in the care of another one of his children. He was keeping watch, even when she made terrible missteps.

Indigo heard her sister take the phone from Sasha. She inhaled deeply to prepare herself for the rest of this conversation. The most important thing Yasmin needed to hear right now was also the only thing Indigo wanted to tell her.

"Indie?" Yasmin said, still sounding ashamed.

"Yas? I love you, baby sis, and I'm in this with you."

36

If this weren't a serious moment and if he weren't in the middle of talking to God, Reuben might have laughed out loud.

Here he was, standing with his family, holding hands for a group prayer led by Pastor Taylor. The pastor was inviting God to be present during this gathering in the living room of the Burns home. Reuben's head was bowed and he was listening to Pastor Taylor, but his thoughts were wandering too.

If someone had told him a year ago that he would chuck a great job on the West Coast for small-town life in Jubilant, Texas, where he'd wind up in private counseling with a minister and a growing interest in a relationship with God, *that* Reuben Burns would have laughed out loud and demanded a breathalyzer test for his so-called prophetic friend.

But this Reuben Burns *was* here. In fact, this one, who couldn't remember the last time he'd had a panic attack or a nightmare, and who didn't miss Wednesday night Bible study unless there was an emergency, was the one who had requested tonight's meeting with Mama, Daddy, Indigo, Max, and Peyton.

Taryn had come to his house to babysit Charles David, and he and Peyton had arrived at Mama's with pizza and salad for dinner, so Mama wouldn't feel compelled to cook. Normally she would have prepared her Sunday meal the day before, but she had been too distraught about Yasmin yesterday.

Pastor Taylor had promised to come over after worship service, once the congregation had left. He rang the doorbell of the Burnses' home at three p.m. sharp, and Indigo led him into the living room, where Mama and Daddy were anxiously awaiting what was to come.

Reuben saw fear and shame in both their eyes and wanted to hug them. He and Indigo hadn't told them specifically why they had asked Pastor Taylor to stop by—just that with all that had happened over the past few days, with Yasmin's pictures circulating throughout the city and Mama contemplating how to handle the Woman of the Year recognition, they needed to have some family time with their minister.

Pastor Taylor launched into a prayer before formally greeting his hosts.

"And dear Lord," he said, wrapping up the petition. "Let us all leave here tonight a little closer to you and kinder to each other, a little less fearful of the unknown and a little more courageous about following where you want to lead. Most of all, Father, let us love more deeply and unconditionally than we imagine is possible. We ask that this be done in our lives and that as we grow and mature into this request, we remember to give you all the glory and the praise for honoring our prayer. Amen."

Pastor Taylor raised his head and grinned. "Now that that's all settled, hello, family!" He opened his arms wide. "Irene. Charles."

Mama allowed him to gather her in an embrace. Daddy extended his hand for a shake first, then grasped the pastor for a hug. He offered Pastor Taylor a seat, and Mama brought him a glass of the iced tea he always requested whenever he dined with the family. She seemed nervous when she sat next to him and placed an envelope on her lap. Everyone else took a seat and stopped chatting.

"I know you're here about Yasmin, Pastor," Mama said in a voice just above a whisper. "I know you've seen the terrible pictures, or at least heard about them. I've already written my resignation letter for that 'Woman of the Year' award. I just hope I haven't embarrassed our church again."

She slipped the folded ivory linen resume paper from the envelope and began to read aloud.

> *While I feel fortunate to have been recognized for my service to the community, it is with sincere respect and regret that I rescind my nomination as The Jubilant Women's Foundation Woman of the Year. For personal reasons, I do not feel qualified to accept the honor at this time. I am hopeful—*

Before she could continue, Reuben rose from his seat and gently tugged the letter from Mama's hand.

"Stop, Mama. You don't have to do that."

Mama looked at her now empty hands and then at Pastor Taylor before addressing Reuben. "But I do. It's hypocritical to be honored for outward success when obviously something is wrong with how I've raised you and your sisters. You and Yasmin took off the minute you could. I don't know why Indigo hasn't left me yet, but I'm probably pushing her out too."

Reuben looked at Indigo, hoping she could steer this conversation back to where it should have been headed. They had agreed to have this meeting to reveal to their parents that Indigo had talked to Yasmin yesterday, and that their younger sister intended to stay in New York.

But Indigo seemed startled by Mama's outburst. Her eyes were riveted on Mama, and she seemed as if she wanted—or needed—to hear more.

Pastor Taylor cleared his throat and looked at Reuben, as if to say, Chill, and follow where God is leading. Reuben took a deep breath and settled back in his seat. Peyton, who sat next to him, patted his thigh, her familiar gesture for comforting him.

"Is there anything else you'd like to say, Irene?" Pastor Taylor asked.

Mama lowered her eyes and shook her head. "No, unless you have some suggestions for my letter."

Pastor Taylor stared at her for a few minutes before speaking. "My only suggestion is that you tear it up. If you can't be Woman of the Year because your family isn't perfect, then none of the previous recipients should have accepted the honor either. They decided to give you the award because of the challenges and mistakes you've overcome, not because your life is 100 percent wonderful.

"You aren't the only mother whose child has run away and broken her heart. You aren't the only mother who has been publicly humiliated by a child she tried to give the best. Maybe now more than ever you need to stand and take this award, for all of those mothers, to show them that at some point we have to give our children to God and trust that as long as we have acquainted them with God and poured the knowledge and power of his love into them, they are equipped to fly right—it's their choice."

Pastor Taylor reared back in his chair and glanced at Daddy. He looked at Reuben again and hesitated.

"May I?"

Reuben's heart stopped. He knew what Pastor Taylor wanted to say, and doing so might take the conversation even further from where Reuben and Indigo had intended. He almost shook his head no, but he had been reading a lot lately about overcoming one's fears, and Max had been talking with him about the importance of speaking the truth in love.

Reuben glanced at Max and saw that his friend was awaiting his response.

"Yes, Pastor," Reuben finally said. "Go where God is leading."

Pastor Taylor turned his body toward Daddy, who sat across the room from him. "Brother Charles, if you don't mind, I'd like to go back to what Sister Irene said a few minutes ago, right after she read the letter. Everything she said was 'I' didn't do this, or 'I' did do that. She didn't acknowledge that there were two of you parenting these grandchildren. Any reason why?"

Daddy sat up straighter and wrung his hands. Reuben knew he hated being put on the spot, especially in front of his entire family. But according to Pastor Taylor, sometimes the hot seat was the only wake-up call a person got.

"She just talks like that," Daddy said in a faltering voice. "She always wants to take the blame for everything."

"If there's any blame, is she the only one who deserves it?" Pastor Taylor asked.

Daddy didn't respond.

"When she was drinking, where were you, Brother Charles? When the children needed someone to talk to, or a parent to make them feel secure, were you here? Who made the final decisions about Yasmin's modeling? Sister Irene?"

"We both did," Daddy choked out. His eyes were downcast, and his shoulders slumped forward.

"I'm not asking these questions to beat you up, Brother Charles," Pastor Taylor said.

Although Daddy hadn't lifted his head, the minister stared at him, lovingly.

"I want you to think about what I'm asking. I want you to hear the guilt your wife is feeling. I want both of you to own your role as parents, and then forgive yourselves for being human.

"Before you can get to the forgiveness, though, you've got to look in the mirror and be real about your human shortcomings. When you accept whatever role you played, or didn't play, you can move forward."

Daddy raised his eyes and looked at Pastor Taylor. "What do you mean, did or didn't play? I was here. I was their father."

Pastor Taylor leaned forward and nodded. Reuben had become so familiar with his body language that he knew Pastor Taylor felt like they were getting somewhere.

"You may have been here physically, but what about emotionally? You had a wife struggling with alcoholism. How did that affect you? Did you check out to keep your sanity? Did you emotionally detach so it wouldn't hurt so much?

"If you did any of those things, were you fully here, parenting and being a husband who made wise decisions and led from the heart, or one who just went through the motions of what you thought a man should do? There is a difference, you know."

Indigo, her eyes filled with tears, turned toward Reuben and mouthed for him to make Pastor Taylor stop. Before Reuben could respond, Max leaned into her and whispered something in her ear.

She wiped a tear from her eye and bit her lip.

Pastor Taylor sat back and looked at everyone in the room. "I'm not trying to get you folks angry tonight, or make you feel bad about yourselves. I'm actually here to discuss Yasmin. But before we can get to the baby of the family and what can be done to help her, we have to look at the foundational issues of how everyone in this room got where they are, alright?"

When no one responded, Pastor Taylor kept talking. "Sister Irene, you pray about what I said earlier and ask God what he wants you to do about that award. Brother Charles, I meant what I said: I'm not trying to beat you up, brother. I just want us all to get real tonight, so that as a family, regardless of where Yasmin winds up, you can start a new chapter in a good place, trusting each other and loving each other at a whole new level. You've got to own who you have been before you can decide to become who God is calling you to be."

Reuben nodded. "Amen, Pastor." He looked from Mama to Daddy and took a deep breath. "Remember the conversation Peyton and I had with you two about how Indigo was feeling, and about how she needed you?"

His parents nodded and he continued. "That wouldn't have happened if I hadn't been working on myself. I've been meeting with Pastor Taylor for a while, to get over issues from my past that we've already talked about. As I've worked on that, I've learned how to get real with myself, so I can be real with God and with other people.

"I know how you may be feeling right now, Daddy," Reuben said. "But going down that uncomfortable path with Pastor Taylor has been the wake-up call I needed. Peyton and Charles David needed me to grow up. I needed me to grow up, and I had to let go of the old me in order to do that."

Pastor Taylor pulled one of his smooth moves to lighten the mood. "Ain't nobody telling you and Sister Irene that your growth is stunted," he said and laughed. Everyone joined him. "Brother

Reuben means he has grown emotionally and spiritually. Everyone's needs and seasons are different—which brings me to why I am here tonight."

Pastor Taylor glanced at Indigo, who sat up straight in her seat. Max draped his arm across her shoulders in support.

"Mama, Daddy, I have something to tell you," she said.

Daddy sat up and looked angry. "I'm not ready to be a great-grandfather again, young lady."

Indigo and Max blushed. "Daddy!"

Pastor Taylor coughed. "Let's try this again. Indigo wants to share some news about Yasmin."

Mama clutched her chest. "Please tell me nothing bad has happened to her! What is it?"

Reuben was beginning to think this was a bad idea. There was no need to drag this out. "Mama—she called Indigo yesterday, after that tabloid newspaper hit the newsstands. She is in New York and she's safe."

There. It was said. Short and simple.

Mama and Daddy looked confused.

"She called you yesterday and you didn't tell me?" Mama said to Indigo. "You know how your daddy and I have been worrying! What's going on, Indigo?"

"Mama, I felt comfortable holding off on talking to you about this because I knew she was okay," Indigo said. "If I had even mentioned that we had talked, you would have wanted to know details. I wanted to not only tell you she was fine, but also prepare you for the decisions she's made."

Indigo paused and Reuben looked at Mama to see if his sister's words were resonating with her.

"Yas is back with Sasha Davies, from Ford Models, and Sasha is already working to clean up this mess with the photos," Indigo said. "Apparently Yasmin was tricked into taking the pictures by a sleazy photographer, so Ford Models is going to make her the poster child for young girls who want to model, to warn them of the dangers of trying to land work without first making sure they are being hired by reputable people."

Mama nodded. "That sounds good. Thank God Sasha wants to help her."

"Why is Ms. Davies doing this, though?" Daddy asked.

"It's a long story," Indigo said. "But basically, Sasha has landed Yas some really good modeling jobs and intends to keep representing Yasmin after this blows over."

Indigo let those words sink in, knowing what was coming next.

"What do you mean, 'after this blows over'?" Daddy asked. "Now that we know where she is, she can just come home and let it blow over."

Indigo glanced at Reuben, and he knew that was his cue.

"That's why we called the meeting tonight, Daddy, to let you and Mama know what Yasmin's wishes are. She is eighteen now and legally doesn't have to come home. And she doesn't want to. She wants to keep living in New York and modeling—not the sleazy stuff she got caught up in, but more work with Ford, which is still interested in grooming her into a supermodel."

Indigo leaned forward. "This is the real deal, Mama and Daddy. They want to take her to the next level, and they are going to, with Yasmin's full agreement. She's not coming home anytime soon. She told me to tell you that she loves you and she has forgiven you for all that happened in the past. She wants you to forgive her for her huge mistake with those semi-nude photos. And for running away and making you worry.

"She says she knew better than to trust that photographer. She felt uncomfortable during the entire shoot. But she didn't know how to get out of it once it started. She asked to stop and the photographer threatened to sue her. She knows you're embarrassed, and she just hasn't worked up the nerve to call you herself and say she's sorry."

Mama looked as if she'd gone into a trance. Daddy was speechless.

"What about school? Her education? You have to have at least a high school degree to work everywhere these days, don't you?"

Indigo nodded. "Sasha works with budding models all the time and has arranged for Yasmin to work with a private tutor this year to obtain the credits she needs to receive her diploma. Basically, she'll be homeschooled, but it will be in sessions with three to four other models."

Daddy shook his head. "I don't know about this. We pulled her out of modeling because we were worried about the influence of those other models, about the terrible things they were doing. I just don't know. She's not old enough for all of this."

"Daddy, apparently she is," Indigo said. "She's been living in New York by herself for the past month. Yes, she made that huge mistake with the one photographer, but she's about to become a star by speaking out about what happened to her. She's going to help so many young girls. Besides, she is eighteen. She has the right to make her own decisions."

Pastor Taylor cleared his throat. "Which brings me back to the reason I was invited here tonight. It goes back to the prayer I uttered when I first entered the room. You as a family need to ask God to give you that unconditional love for Yasmin, even when you don't agree with her choices, or you may lose her forever. You need to ask God to help you trust more, so that in trusting him, you can surrender your fears about the parts of Yasmin's journey that you don't understand.

"I know this isn't easy," Pastor Taylor said. "But remember that we are just stewards of the children God gives us. We have the privilege of shepherding them up to a certain point, and then we have to lean on God to guide them and keep them the rest of the way."

Indigo nodded. "If it makes you feel any better, I had a long talk with Sasha, and she's really got a good heart, Mama and Daddy. She's going to look out for Yasmin because of her commitment to her faith."

A single tear slipped down Mama's cheek and she bowed her head. "Praise God for that. Lord, please surround my baby with angels and keep her safe. And let her come home again, please, God. I can't take losing another child for a decade."

Reuben's heart ripped in two. He realized for the first time how much pain he had caused. He didn't feel guilty for staying away in his effort to take care of himself; Pastor Taylor had helped him clarify that. What he felt horrible about was not sharing his truths sooner, to help his parents/grandparents and his sisters understand why he needed his space. That information would have been enough to make some difference.

Reuben hoped by starting off with the truth, Yasmin's flight from the coop would be very different from his own.

"I haven't talked to her yet," he told his parents, "but I don't think Yasmin's going to need to stay away as long as I did. As long as she can come home without having to fight to be who she is, she will return to us often."

Indigo nodded and smiled. She looked at Mama. "She has already asked Sasha to clear her calendar so she can be here when you receive your Woman of the Year award."

37

Mama and Indigo sat in front of the computer, visiting women's clothing websites to find the perfect dress for Mama. She needed something fabulous to wear in the photo she would submit soon for the promotional media tied to her upcoming award.

Indigo was going to shoot the photo in Max's studio and wanted Mama to buy something vibrant and elegant that said "Wow!"

It was Sunday afternoon, and everyone had left after dinner except Indigo. Max had wished the two women happy shopping and had gone home to take a nap.

Indigo was bookmarking a site with a royal purple ruffled gown she liked when Mama touched her arm.

"I'm sorry, Indie," she said.

Indigo tried to quell her surprise.

"I've taken you for granted for way too long. I've checked out on your wedding planning and on just about anything that wasn't related to Reuben and his family."

Indigo knew her shock registered in her eyes. For a few seconds, she thought she might have imagined the comment.

Mama gave her a sad smile. "I've received more than one wake-up call this week. Sometimes God has to kick you in the teeth to get your attention. He has mine now, and so do you. I'm sorry about your wedding. What have you decided?"

"We considered several options before deciding. We're going to Jamaica, Mama," Indigo said.

Mama did a double take. "I had heard you were considering that but didn't think you were serious."

Indigo nodded and grinned. "There are a number of reasons why, including Yasmin's absence. But the real reason is beautiful. You should see what we're trying to buy instead."

Mama smiled and slid her feet into her low-heeled slides, which were right next to her computer chair. "Show me."

Now it was Indigo's turn to be stunned. "Right now?"

"Right now. Me and your daddy."

A few minutes later, with Mama and Daddy buckled into the backseat of her Jetta, Indigo drove through the Aldersgate Landing subdivision, down the street she was hopeful would become familiar territory. She parked in front of the house she and Max were working toward securing and climbed out of the car. Mama and Daddy stepped out too and stood on the sidewalk in front of the home.

The realtor wasn't there today, so they couldn't go inside. But Mama and Daddy still got enough of a view to be impressed. They walked around to the backyard so Daddy could check out the potential for landscaping.

"We figured we'd take the bulk of the money from the wedding expenses and use it for this, along with proceeds from the sale of Max's home," Indigo said. "We want to keep our mortgage as low as possible, so we can live comfortably despite the ebb and flow of clients in our business."

Mama looked at her. "Did you say 'our' business?"

Indigo nodded and smiled. "A couple of months ago Max was

trying to convince me to become co-owner of his photography studio, since we were getting married. I was on the fence and he sensed my ambivalence. Max backed off the idea, mostly for my sake. I was relieved, but I kept asking God about it. Slowly but surely, I realized how much time I was spending there anyway, and God gave me a peace about moving forward."

Indigo and her parents headed back toward the car. "I asked Max to reconsider and brotherman was beside himself. We're having legal documents drawn up to protect each of our interests, outside of the marriage."

Mama shook her head and opened her arms to hug Indigo. "You amaze me, young lady."

Daddy was still eyeing the house. "When will you guys sign?"

"Oh, I don't know yet, Daddy. We're trying to put as much down as we can, so unless we hear that there's some competition, we'll save for a few more weeks."

All three of them were silent on the ride back to Mama and Daddy's house. Indigo was dying to know what they thought of the decisions she had made without their guidance, but she didn't have the nerve to ask. She wondered if they were fretting over her choices, or maybe lost in thought on something entirely different.

Indigo pulled into the driveway behind Mama's Toyota and they entered through the kitchen. She headed back to the computer room to resume exploring the sites she and Mama wanted to check out, but Daddy stopped her before she turned the corner.

"Come here for a minute, Indie."

He perched on a stool positioned near the granite island and motioned for Indigo to sit on the one next to him. Mama took a seat at the nearby kitchen table and waited for Daddy to speak.

Daddy pulled his checkbook from his back pocket and laid it

on the island countertop so he could write. He tore off two checks and placed them in Indigo's hand.

Her eyes widened. "What are you doing?"

"You've talked about being a bride and having a fairytale wedding since you were a little girl. I would never forgive myself if you didn't follow through on that dream," he said, gazing at her. He leaned toward her to stroke her cheek and kiss her forehead. "You're still my little girl, you know? I haven't always done the best job of telling you how much I care about you, or how important your hopes and dreams are to me, but I want you to know that I do care, and I want you to be happy.

"Your mama and I have been intending to pitch in and help with your wedding expenses all along. I'm sorry we were too preoccupied to follow through on that. That first check should cover the bulk of your needs."

Indigo gasped when she viewed the amount. She looked from the check into her father's eyes several times. His gray mustache rose at the sides as he grinned at her disbelief.

"Daddy—you're retired! Don't you need this?"

He shook his head. "We've been planning for your special day for a long time, Princess. It was already set aside. And just so you know, your parents helped with this too. A portion of this check, and the funds we used to pay for your college expenses, came from the insurance policies we received after their deaths."

Indigo couldn't speak. She waved the other check in the air, stunned by the zeroes it contained as well.

"Consider that one our wedding gift," he said. "Use that toward the down payment on your new home, if you want."

Daddy must have noted her skepticism.

"We're not trying to buy your love, Indigo," he said. "We've been doing a lot of praying and reflecting, and we're finally owning up to our mistakes. There are a lot of good things about our family, but there are areas we need to work on. Being there for each other, through thick and thin, is one of them. Your mama and I want to start with you, as you plan for your future."

Indigo shook her head. She wasn't dreaming. God had answered her prayers for a breakthrough with her parents. This was beyond any scenario she had imagined.

At some point in the near future, she would express to them how little the money meant compared to having their support and interest in her life. For now, the most she could say were the words that kept coursing through her spirit.

"Thank you, Daddy." She uttered the gratitude to both her father/grandfather and to God. Then she turned her eyes toward Mama. "Thank you, both."

38

Reuben told Indigo the truth this morning, after she and Max shared breakfast with him and Peyton.

His sister knew everything now—how Mom had been concerned about her and Yasmin, the promise he had been asked to keep, his reason for returning to Jubilant, and how the nightmares had stopped in recent weeks, since he had been living authentically and giving God a chance.

He was relieved. "I wanted to share this with you this morning, because Pastor Taylor has asked me to give my testimony during worship service today," Reuben said. "I talked with Mama and Daddy about all of this last night."

Indigo raised an eyebrow. Her expression said it all: since when had he been into giving testimonies? He glanced at the clock and tried to snuff out the nervousness trying to surface in his belly. Church would begin in an hour.

"I wish I had more time to tell you how I got talked into doing this," he said. "We'll save that story for this afternoon."

Indigo pushed back her chair and leaned across the table to hug him. "We've got plenty of time for that. Thank you, though, for this morning. I needed to hear what you shared about the accident and Mom Meredith. I'm sorry I've misjudged you."

Reuben shook his head. "No need to apologize. We're coming to the table from different angles and with different perspectives. Just because my experience wasn't the same as yours doesn't mean yours isn't as relevant. Your wounds hurt just as much as mine."

Ninety minutes later, Reuben reiterated that message before the congregation at St. Peter's Baptist. He turned to Pastor Taylor and saw that even he was in tears.

"This day has been a long time coming," Reuben said. "The only one who saw it on the horizon was the one person who wasn't looking with human eyes, because she couldn't. I believe that's part of the reason God sent me Peyton Elise Burns. She looked beyond my faults and she saw the heart of God in me—long before I knew it could be reawakened."

Reuben smiled at his wife and wanted her to know. "I'm smiling at you, Peyt, and I love you."

"Right back at ya, babe," she called out to him.

The congregation hooted and applauded.

He turned to the pianist and motioned with his head that he was ready.

Reuben closed his eyes and wrapped both hands around the microphone. "Ya'll bear with me, now," he said as the music rose to a crescendo. "I haven't sung publicly since I was twelve years old, at the church my family had just begun attending in New Orleans. My dad had just rededicated his life to God, and he played sax every Sunday. Mom sang in the choir, and one time, she and I did a duet."

Reuben opened his eyes and looked at Mama and Daddy, who were seated in the second row. Mama was already dabbing her moist eyes with tissues. Daddy bit his lip in an effort to maintain his composure.

"The last time I actually sang a full song was on the day of the accident, when my mother was trying to help me nail a Stevie Wonder tune. I thought my song had died that day too. But as I've been reading the Scriptures and allowing people like Pastor Taylor and my soon-to-be brother-in-law Max Shepherd speak into my life, I've realized that the song didn't die—I smothered it. So I'm lifting my voice today to honor everything that was sleeping inside and everything that God is restoring."

Reuben launched into Richard Smallwood's *Center of My Joy* and let the tears flow as he sang.

> Jesus, you're the center of my joy . . .
> All that's good and perfect comes from you . . .

He didn't see the river of tears flowing from every eye, or feel Pastor Taylor stand beside him and touch his shoulder, or see Indigo with her head bowed, praying for God to guide him through this song.

As he sang, he saw his mother—Meredith Hill Burns—smiling from heaven, nodding that yes, he had hit the right notes, and that yes, he was a good man.

He saw his dad—David Robert Burns—brimming with pride over the fact that he had come full circle and turned his heart back to God before it was too late.

Reuben saw Yasmin—somewhere feeling lonely this morning, but hopeful, and he knew he had to comfort her. He knew God would lead the family to embrace her so that she too could sing a new song.

He wanted to shout instead of sing, but in obedience, he let the song flow, and every time he tried to wrap it up, someone in the congregation would sing the chorus again.

This day and this testimony were bigger than him and his

fears. He understood that his homecoming had really been about everyone else in the room getting healed too.

There was a lull in the song, where he allowed the music to take over rather than his voice. The instrumental version caused just as much praise to ring out in the church as his singing had. He smiled through his tears and hummed into the microphone.

Thank you, God, for this day, he said in his heart. *Thank you for loving me enough to allow me to keep my promise to Mom and to learn to love you like Peyton has always prayed. This day is for you, and for her.*

Later, after service, he had been inundated by members who wanted to encourage him to sing more and possibly join the church choir. Reuben was flattered, but didn't make promises.

Peyton, Mama, Daddy, Aunt Melba, and the rest of the family sat in a back corner of the church and waited for him to chat with everyone who wanted a minute of his time.

After he hugged the last person in the line and encouraged her to keep trusting God, he dug his hands into the pockets of his gray slacks and strolled over to the group.

"Is the rock star ready to go?" Peyton said and grinned.

Reuben leaned over and kissed her lips. "Is this legal in church, other than when you're getting married?"

"Too late to be asking now," Peyton said. She stood up and wrapped an arm around his waist.

Pastor Taylor waved as the family left through the front door. "Y'all look mighty good!" he said. "Keep holding on to each other."

Indigo and Reuben exchanged glances. She looked at her watch.

"In a few more hours I'm praying we'll look even better," she said.

Reuben stepped toward Indigo and gathered her in his arms. He kissed her cheek. "No need to hope—we *will*."

The brother and sister had booked a flight from Houston to New York, where they would spend a week with Yasmin. She was still living with Sasha Davies, and they were going to stay at a nearby hotel.

They would travel bearing gifts—a letter of reconciliation from Mama and Daddy, a gift-wrapped box that bore a key to their house, and an invitation to still serve as the maid of honor in Indigo's wedding, if Yasmin's modeling schedule permitted. The entire family, but especially Mama and Daddy, wanted Yasmin to know that wherever she decided to live and whatever opportunities she pursued, she always had a place in their hearts and she always had a home in Jubilant.

Reuben and Indigo's top priority during the visit would be to let Yasmin know that the Burnses were changing, for the better. She needed to see firsthand that healing had taken place between the two of them, and she deserved to be part of the process.

Reuben and Indigo wanted to help her soar, no matter how much patience, forgiveness, and courage it took. That's what dreams were all about, they had agreed, considering how their own had taken shape. If Yasmin could make hers a reality sooner rather than later, they would do everything they could to help her succeed.

DISCUSSION QUESTIONS

1. What was the primary theme of this novel and how did that resonate with you?
2. Was Indigo's lingering anger at Reuben understandable, or did she come across as a brat?
3. Was it realistic that Reuben would feel guilty about a promise made when he was a child?
4. How could Irene and Charles Burns have better handled Reuben's return to Jubilant?
5. Did Indigo appropriately handle her parents' routine disregard of her needs?
6. What was the biggest problem facing this family? What triggered the resolution?
7. Is it typical for a family to have secrets and skeletons that they don't want to confront? How does hiding issues like this keep a family from thriving?
8. How would you have handled Yasmin's eighteenth birthday decision?
9. Was Max a good role model for Reuben? How so?

10. Was it surprising that Indigo stayed in contact with Brian? How did this help both of them heal?
11. Were Reuben's conversations with his parents about their mistakes warranted?
12. What purpose did Peyton serve in the story? What did she symbolize?
13. Was Pastor Taylor's counseling and mentoring of Reuben enough to help him heal, or should more have been done?
14. What did you think of Yasmin's decision at the end of the book? Did her parents handle it appropriately?
15. Was the reconciliation between Reuben and Indigo authentic?
16. What messages or characters will linger with you from this book?

ACKNOWLEDGMENTS

Birthing books is often like birthing children—each one is unique yet special, and each one is crafted through its own particular journey. The road to finishing this project was challenging yet memorable, and it couldn't have been accomplished without my steadfast team of support: my husband, Donald, and our two thoughtful children; my wonderful editors, Lonnie Hull Dupont and Barb Barnes; and my first readers, Carol Jackson and Sharon Shahid. Thank you for helping me share yet another story and message that I hope resonates with readers far and wide.

A special thanks is issued, as always, to my mentor and special friend, Muriel Miller Branch, for your unconditional love and encouragement and for providing my writing haven any time I need.

I also sincerely thank my siblings, Dr. Barbara Grayson, Henry Haney, Sandra Williams, and Patsy Scott; along with Teresa Coleman, Linda Beed, Marilynn Griffith, Michelle McKinney Hammond, Claudia Mair Burney, Sibella Giorello, Tyora Moody, Carol Mackey, Michele Misiak, Johanna Schuchert, Kia Short Lee, Lauren Stewart, Danielle Jones, Kyle Grinnage, Sally Ribeiro,

Katrina Campbell, Gwendolyn Richard, Barbara Rascoe, Shaun Robinson, the Adams family, Helena Nyman, Gloria Thomas, Rhonda McKnight, Dee Stewart, Sherri Lewis, Nan McDonald, Connie and Ernest Lambert and family, Charmaine Spain, the Murphy family, and my extended body of friends and family throughout Richmond.

As always, I am grateful for the support of my agent, Steve Laube, the marketing and sales team at Revell Books, booksellers, book clubs, and book reviewers and bloggers who continue to sell and tout my books. Thanks to you, I'm able to keep sharing the stories in my heart.

I thank you, the individual reader, for supporting my work and encouraging others to read as well. I pray that this story, as well as others I've penned, inspires you on your journey and leaves you yearning to know God more deeply.

And in the effort to save the best for last, I offer a heartfelt thanks to my gracious and loving heavenly Father, for giving me the gift of writing and the opportunity to be used in service to Him through my books.

Blessings always,
Stacy

Stacy Hawkins Adams is an award-winning author, journalist, and inspirational speaker. She and her family live in a suburb of Richmond, Virginia. Her other published titles include *Speak to My Heart*, *Nothing but the Right Thing*, *Watercolored Pearls*, and the first two books in the Jubilant Soul series, *The Someday List* and *Worth a Thousand Words*. She welcomes readers to visit her website: www.stacyhawkinsadams.com.